Feta and the Fat Bastard

Judy Volhart

Open Books

Published by Open Books

ISBN-13: 978-0615722870

Prologue

She was upset and on a rampage. Her long blonde hair clung to a tear-streaked face while she threw things around in the kitchen, ferociously preparing their salads with a vengeance.

How dare he treat her so callously?! After all she did for him and put up with? She cringed, remembering the feel of his rough and heavy hands groping her, the feel of his immense, sweating body and the old, jowly flesh swaying above her.

Oh, he had nerve all right!

After all these years, to still be treated like his toy, like a nobody, and having put up with it, waiting, patiently waiting, for him to die, sure that his old, fat heart would soon give out.

Well, it wasn't soon enough, and she'd have to find a way to speed things up.

Chapter One

I huffed and I puffed then stumbled and fell backward onto my behind, jarring my tailbone and blinking rapidly to clear the stars that filled my eyes. I lay on the ground and fought the overwhelming urge to cry, so reminiscent of the first day that I had moved here, roughly five months earlier.

Through bleary eyes, I looked up at the crystal blue sky. The month of May in Ottawa can be absolutely stunning, and I soon snapped out of my mood as the spring sun warmed and caressed my skin, gently soothing my spirit. I closed my eyes for a moment, enjoying the late spring heat.

I was still in this graceless position, however, when I noticed two sets of beady eyes staring down at me. Hark, the Aliens!

Oh, you know by now that they're not really aliens. I just affectionately call my parents that because they're so...so...non-North American. They're stuck in 1960s Hungary and haven't evolved with the times very much. The only reason they even own a microwave is because I recently bought them one, but my father refuses to use it due to safety concerns, like radiation.

"*Alszol?*" my mom jokingly asked, gently prodding me with a foot.

"No, I'm not sleeping. I fell when I was bringing out the Oleander plant and got winded. I'm okay now." I stood up and brushed myself off, screeching when I found a weird electric blue bug clinging to my cinnamon – colored hair and slapping myself silly in my insane attempt to dislodge it.

Ah yes, cinnamon. It used to be a delicious caramel color, but I recently discovered a number of silver hairs on my still thirty-year-old head, no doubt as a result of some very stressful months of late. Feeling adventurous, I had intended to stray just ever so slightly from my normal box of color. I had purchased one that promised me light, golden caramel hair, but in my case, it turned cinnamon. After a couple of days, though, I had decided that I rather liked the reddish tinge and had gotten many compliments on it. In truth, I was also too lazy to change it.

My name is Amalia Kis. Welcome to my bistro, the Whine and Cheese. The bistro part is on the main floor of the building I own while my living quarters are above. I moved here five months earlier and luckily business was going well, otherwise I'd be out of both a job and a home and I would likely have to move back in with the Aliens, who conveniently (for them) now lived just a couple of minutes away from me.

I do love them, but in all honesty, I loved them more when they lived over two hours away in Montreal, rather than just two minutes away. Too close for my comfort.

My parents helped me finish moving the large Oleander into position and then helped me bring the second one out. Soon, both plants were on either side of the front entrance to the bistro, giving it a homey feeling. I imagined them stretching their limbs luxuriously in the sunshine after being cooped up inside my office all winter, and thanking me in their silent plant way.

I also had just enough room for three patio chairs on the small front porch where my parents and I proceeded to sit with three glasses and a bottle of wine.

Since I abhor pretentiousness, the bistro sells only wines with quirky names and this one was no exception. We each took a long sip from our glass of Project Happiness. The big yellow happy face on the bottle made me smile and the taste of the fruity Syrah wine with hints of black cherry, blackberries and spices enveloping my tongue made me relish being alive.

Only one thing could make it better. I leaned forward and snagged a thin sliver of spicy Hungarian salami off the platter on the little glass table between us and munched in contentment. Although I like many salamis sliced thick, this one is best sliced paper thin due to its heat.

"So, what brings you by?" I finally asked my parents.

"We were hoping that you and Mutt could come over one day and help us with the pool. Some of the pool fence came loose during the winter and the liner has slipped a little too." They still pronounced Matt's name as *Mutt*, and I couldn't help but giggle as the wine hit my almost-empty belly then bee-lined straight to my head.

"Sure, I'll ask Mutt if he's free anytime soon and give you a call later this week." Matt has been my boyfriend for the past four months and still makes the little hairs on my toes curl. I had been single for about two years before meeting him, and with his Keith Urban looks, he kept my libido longing for more. After having been in a six-year relationship with Hans, who loved only his money and himself, and then single for two years, my libido deserved a little attention, thank you very much.

As if sensing my thoughts, Hans pulled his car into my lot and drove nearly up to the front door. I bared my teeth and hissed as he got out of the car and strode toward us.

Over six feet tall, Hans tossed his perfectly coiffed blond hair and greeted my parents as though they were long lost friends. Jaws agape, they looked at me in surprise. I quickly told them in Hungarian that he periodically came by to torment me.

My father glared openly at him while my mother mumbled a cool but polite hello. It was so garbled that I couldn't tell in which language she had responded.

"How are you doing, Mr. and Mrs. Kis? I haven't seen you in so long. What a wonderful surprise!" Hans purred with fake politeness and threw his arms open wide, expecting hugs. My dad wasn't having any of it since he never particularly thought highly of him in the first place, nor was my father one to hold his tongue.

"Vat you doing here, veasle? Go avay, ve having notting to saying to you. Go!" My dad exclaimed in his broken English while making shooing motions as he shot out of his chair. After a speechless moment, Hans huffed and turned on his heel. Before getting back into his car, he threw a smirk my way then slammed his door and peeled out of the lot, sending bits of gravel flying and my temper flaring.

I had come to the conclusion that his mission in life was to boil my blood. Our relaxed mood spoiled, my parents left soon after and I went in to start preparing the food as it was almost opening time for the bistro.

Nicole and one of my new helpers, Beth, arrived at the same time. They came in through the heavy, steel back door, walked through my office and into the kitchen area where I was elbow deep in chopped veggies for the salads that we were serving, now that winter was finally over and everyone was craving greens.

Personally, I wasn't much of a salad fan, although today's special was an exception. Mixed greens with strawberries, toasted slivered almonds, fresh chives that had already sprouted in my small, eclectic garden, a homemade raspberry-garlic vinaigrette and the pièce de resistance, a lovely, creamy, low sodium feta cheese. I sneaked a piece of it and popped it into my mouth, letting it sit on my tongue a moment before chomping into its saltiness.

The daily hot dish, taco-style chicken, was simmering on the stove in a giant pot and the staples of my bistro, the cheeses and salamis, were pre-sliced and ready for quick platter preparation.

Nicole had been my best friend since the age of twelve and was in every way my opposite. She was a tiny, graceful blond with green eyes, a dance instructor, and also had a killer voice. Between waiting tables, she would take the stage and croon jazz songs to the delight of my customers.

My other close friends, Nora and Chloé, also helped out at the bistro, but tonight each needed the night off for various family functions. Beth was new to our little team, the result of my somewhat booming business. It was also a necessity to ensure that I was fully staffed as my hours of operation would soon be expanding and because the existing staff had summer vacations planned.

Beth was stunning, with long muscular legs that went on forever and ebony hair that hung down to her waist. Today she had it up in a neat bun, but even with her old-fashioned look and retro-style black rimmed glasses, you could still tell that she was a beauty. She had started two weeks earlier, answering my crude homemade sign at the side of the road advertising for a position. So far, she seemed to fit in perfectly with my little gang.

I greeted both with a glass of the happy-face wine, just to finish the bottle, of course. It would be a tragedy if it went stale, and what good would it be owning a wine bistro if I couldn't drink it myself? It was one of the perks.

We sipped as we went around the bistro, lighting the red and black candles on the tables. The ambiance I had created was sleek but laid back and casual, with vibrant red and subdued mocha walls, brownish-black furniture, glossy, red tables and comfortable club chairs and couches. Other than the pizza joint a couple of miles away, my bistro was the only place at this end of town to go out for a bite, and I had taken great care to make it both inviting and classy.

With the candles lit, we emptied our glasses and then opened the front door for business. There was a couple already sitting on the porch, enjoying the sun and the breeze. For some reason, I was surprised, but I supposed I shouldn't be. Although this was also my home, to my customers it was just a place of business, and no doubt they thought the patio chairs were there for them to enjoy. In fact, this couple even requested that I bring out two salads and a small platter of salami and cheese, along with a bottle of wine for them to enjoy outside.

"Whatever is good in your little place here, white this time" was my only instruction in reference to the wine selection. I did not take offence to their tone; they had been here a few times before, and I recalled their dismissive attitude. Nevertheless, I sighed silently to myself and made a mental note to remove the chairs during business hours. I really didn't like the infringement on my personal space.

I returned shortly with a bottle of Arrogant Frog, inspired by the old man's holier-than-thou attitude, his bulgy eyes and massive jowls. The last time they were here and had left the wine choice to me I had served them a bottle of Bad Attitude. Snickering silently, I poured each a glassful then placed the bottle on the table between them with an ever-so-sweet smile and promised to return shortly with their food.

When the choice is left to me, I select the wine based on my mood or impression of the customer. It's my private laugh at the world, and it amuses me to no end.

A number of other customers had now arrived, so while I prepared platters in the kitchen, Nicole and Beth looked after seating and taking orders.

"Beth, can you take this out to the couple on the porch please?" I pointed to the two strawberry and feta salads along with the small platter of meats and cheeses.

"My pleasure," she chirped, already well on her way with those long legs.

She was just about to go out onto the porch when the old man blustered inside. She gave him a cheery smile which froze when he looked beyond her and let the door slam behind him, despite the fact that she was standing there with her hands full. She muttered to herself under her breath as he made his way to the restroom.

Putting the salads down on an empty table near the door, she first brought the platter out then returned for the salads. On her way back inside, she almost collided with frog-man again, and he scowled fiercely. "Excuse me, sir," she mumbled, stepping aside to let him pass as he lumbered by her with a grunt.

The patio chair protested slightly as he heaved his girth back onto it. Smacking his lips, he picked up his salad. "This rabbit food looks better than that wilted crap we have at home," he said. He was just about to take a bite when his young wife squealed, effectively stopping his fork in mid-air. He raised his brow at her.

"Everything okay, Blanche?"

"Oh, Milton, you *must* switch salads with me. Just look at how many strawberries are in yours. Darling, you know how much I adore strawberries." She threw him a sexy pout and he sneered at her, remembering what they had done with strawberries just the night before. Oh, yes, he knew how much she adored those berries!

"Of course, my dear," he replied as he switched bowls with her. They ate in silence, the thirty-year difference in age a significant communication barrier. Milton preferred it that way, anyway. If her mouth was full, then he wouldn't have to listen to her incessant babble.

Just then, a booming voice growled his name:

"Milton! The fat bastard that lost millions for me! Honestly, Milt, I'd hoped you were dead by now!" He then turned to Blanche. "My apologies, Blanche. I hope at least that you're well." His eyes softened when she smiled at him.

Milton turned his head toward the voice, his fleshy face screwed up as though he had smelled dog-do. "Pig-headed fool! I told you to cash in your investments, but you wouldn't listen. You have no one to blame but yourself. And if I recall, it was closer to one million, and that's hardly worth noting."

"You'll get what you deserve, you fat bastard." The lanky man took one step forward, his fists balled tightly at his sides.

"Greg, leave him be. Let's just go inside." The pretty blonde at his side laid a hand on his arm and tugged slightly after giving Blanche an almost imperceptible nod. With a polite nod at Blanche, Greg slowly trailed behind his wife, still muttering under his breath.

"Fool!" Milton chuckled to his wife, not the least bit ruffled over the incident.

"Honestly, darling, you should have some compassion. Poor Greg was accustomed to a certain lifestyle and now he has to *work* for a living. I'm sure it can't be easy." Blanche's chide was met with a contemptuous snort.

They finished their food and wine just as the evening began to chill. Beth appeared, asking if they'd like anything else and Milton shook his heavy face. "Just the bill," he said.

"Right away, sir," Beth replied, unable to fight the urge to use a phony British accent. Although he didn't notice, it didn't escape his wife, who looked up in surprise and allowed a subtle smile to escape.

"Milton, darling, you really should be more polite," she chastised him once Beth was out of earshot. He waved her off with a leathery, fleshy hand.

"I didn't get rich by being polite, Blanche, and I'm sure you wouldn't have married me for my manners."

Beth returned with the bill and Milton tipped her just two dollars for her efforts. Nonetheless, she smiled sweetly and wished them a pleasant evening. As Blanche passed by her, she pressed a twenty-dollar bill into Beth's hand. "Thank you. It was a lovely meal," she whispered.

Milton was already heading purposefully toward their car. Blanche hurried to catch up with him, marveling that someone so large could move so fast. She had almost caught up to him when, without warning, she lurched then fell to the ground.

"Hurry up, Blanche. I'd like to get home in time to watch the play-offs," Milton grumbled over his shoulder. "Blanche?" He turned, annoyed that she did not respond. "What now?" he exclaimed, huffing his way over to her. "Too much booze?" he accused while standing over her. "Get up! You're embarrassing me."

He looked around uneasily, but no one was watching them. "Blanche?"

Crouching, he shook her roughly. "Blanche, stop horsing around."

Finally, he reached a hand to her neck, placing two meaty fingers on her carotid artery, certain that she would squeal with delight that he'd fallen for her trick.

Milton's face registered shock as he felt no pulse.

Feta and Greens

- 2 cups mixed greens of your choice (I often buy the already mixed type in a plastic container. Make sure it has spinach)

- 10 large strawberries, washed, trimmed and cut in half

- 1/2 cup of slivered almonds

- 1/2 cup raspberry vinaigrette salad dressing (such as Kraft)

- 1 tablespoon honey mustard (optional)

- 1 clove minced garlic

- fresh chives (optional – I just happen to have them in my garden)

- 1/2 cup crumbled feta

Prep:

In a 325 degree oven, toast the slivered almonds, watching carefully until they just start to turn golden. Remove immediately from the pan and allow to cool on a plate.

For the salad dressing: you can use the vinaigrette on its own, but mix it with the minced garlic, or you can also mix in the honey mustard. This gives it a fabulous flavor and I highly recommend it.

To serve:

Mix the greens and strawberries. Only when you're ready to eat, pour on the dressing (you may not need all of it—you don't want it to drown!). Then top with slivered almonds, chives and the feta. This is also excellent with sliced, grilled chicken or steak.

Chapter Two

The door burst open and the fat man stumbled inside. "Help, somebody help! Call nine-one-one!" He leaned over, panting. "My wife..." he gasped, trying to catch his breath.

"We'll be right there, sir!" Nicole replied, her arms full of platters, then turned to Beth. "Get Mali and call for help." Beth darted into the kitchen as Nicole rushed to serve the platters. The customers gawked at the commotion.

"Mali, come quickly, something's happened to the old guy's wife!" Beth exclaimed. She then got out her phone to call nine-one-one. Her hands trembled almost uncontrollably.

"Frog man?" I replied before I could stop myself, surprising Beth.

"Yeah, I guess."

We ran out to the lot and I stopped abruptly when I saw Blanche lying on the ground. Instinctively, I reached out an arm to hold Beth back. "Wait here, Beth." I looked back and saw that Milton was almost right next to me and I could hear Beth talking on the phone, conveying to someone at the other end that a woman was lying on the ground.

"I don't think she's breathing," Milton whispered, his face ashen. He glanced again at his watch then scowled, returning his attention to Blanche.

"She's awfully young," I said. "Does she have any medical conditions?"

At first, a rather blank look crossed his face, then he said, "I think she had some sort of infection and was on antibiotics. She was low on something too… what was it? She ate lots of bananas, too. She said that helped her…I don't know—I can't think about all that right now."

Potassium, I thought, but that insight was of no help now. "Is she diabetic? I asked. I knew what to do in cases of diabetic shock.

"She is diabetic," he said, "but I know that she tested her blood sugar just before we came here, and it was in range."

My own hands were trembling since my fingers had just confirmed that she had no pulse.

"Sir, do you mind if I try CPR?" Luckily I had taken a refresher course not long ago, renewing my certification just before I opened my bistro. He bobbed his head frantically. "Yes, yes, do it! What are you waiting for?"

As I moved into position, I noticed him glancing at his watch again. He closed his eyes and sighed deeply. His breath had steadied now, but he still looked ashen.

I hoped the paramedics would arrive without delay otherwise I'd be doing CPR on two people!

I caught Beth's eye and cocked my head toward Milton, meaning for her to try to distract him, but instead she backed away, eyes wide. I didn't have time to analyze her reaction though, and I slowly breathed a few breaths into the lifeless young woman in front of me.

I had been at it for only a few minutes before help arrived. Relieved, I left Blanche in the hands of professionals as I got up on shaky legs, joining Milton and now noticing that Beth had disappeared. The paramedics were loading Blanche into the ambulance when the police arrived, and I knew before he even opened the door that luck wouldn't be on my side, and I mentally braced myself for *him*. Sure enough, he got out of his cruiser and ambled toward me, his new partner trailing a few paces behind.

He nodded and scowled. He should have known my name by now, but he rudely refused to address me accordingly.

"Officer Sean," I said, baring clenched teeth and hoping it passed for a smile. Judging by the slight falter of his scowl, I doubted I was successful but didn't particularly care.

Out of loyalty to Nicole, I couldn't bring myself to be nice to this cop. He had broken her heart and cheated on her, and then stalked her after she had refused to get back together with him. It had only ended after a little help from Matt and his friend

Rick, who'd videotaped Sean's crazy intrusiveness and threatened to go to his chief if he didn't leave her alone. So far, the blackmail was working.

"Care to tell me what happened?" He looked at me expectantly but I shrugged and turned my head toward Milton.

"I have to go with my wife," he said gruffly, turning to get into the back of the ambulance with Blanche.

"I'll see you at the hospital, sir. Wait there for me," Officer Sean said to his back, and then turned his attention to me. I shrugged again.

"They were eating and drinking outside on my veranda, and then she collapsed in the parking lot. He came running inside calling for help, so I ran outside, and after confirming that she had no pulse, I asked for his permission to do CPR."

"What did they eat and drink?" he asked, scribbling on his notepad.

"A strawberry and feta salad, some cheese and salami and they shared a bottle of white wine. It might not be the healthiest food, but surely it didn't have enough time to clog her arteries," I joked feebly. I heard his partner snicker.

Remaining serious, Officer Sean rose a well-trained brow. "Was either acting unusual in any way?"

I scowled. Both were naturally rather unusual, in their own ways. "They've been here before. I can't say that they acted any differently than they did during their previous visits."

He nodded to his partner who appeared to be

quite a pretty young woman. I instantly felt sorry for her, figuring it was just a matter of time before he hit on her, too. "Let's go inside and see if anyone saw or heard anything." She nodded and they headed toward the door while I hung back a little, scouting the parking lot and putting a finger on my twitching pseudo-aneurism that throbbed above my left eye.

I stared vacantly at the spot where I'd given Blanche CPR and tried to push aside the sadness I felt for her. So young, and to have been married to Milton… It was beyond me, but I supposed she had her reasons, and maybe she had really loved him.

I searched the ground looking for any type of clue then slowly walked back to the bistro. Nothing appeared out of the ordinary, no weapons, no trail of blood. Of course, she hadn't appeared injured. It seemed that she had literally just dropped dead. I felt a twinge of hope. Maybe this time it wouldn't be murder. Maybe it was just a natural death.

I walked back inside the bistro, noting that the female cop was now questioning the customers. I had barely closed the door behind me when a slender man and a blonde woman bumped into me while trying to get around me. "Hey, you two, sit back down!" the female cop barked in their direction. "Nobody leaves until I've spoken with you. Sir, you have not spoken with me yet. Sit!"

They slunk back to their table, both of their faces flaming red with embarrassment. I thought I heard the blonde mutter "I told you so" but I wasn't positive. I didn't have time to ponder it though as I caught sight of Beth, looking quite unnerved while she manned the bar area. I made my way over to her.

"How are you holding up?" I asked softly, carefully watching her face for signs of shock.

"I can't believe this is happening!" she hissed back at me. "That lady was nice. If anyone should have dropped dead, it's that nasty man." Her eyes welled with tears. "May I leave?" she asked.

I shook my head. "Not until you've given your statement to the cops, Beth. You waited on them this evening, so they'll definitely want every detail." I didn't think it was possible but she paled even further. I gave her hand a squeeze. "It'll be okay. I'll stay with you." She nodded, swiping angrily at the tears sliding down her cheek. "Why don't you go into the kitchen and wait there? I'll watch the bar." She nodded gratefully and didn't stick around for me to change my mind.

Nicole joined me, her eyes glued to the female cop. "Recognize her?" she asked, a corner of her lip raised in a sneer.

I looked more closely, having given her just a quick glance earlier. She looked slightly familiar, but I couldn't place her. I shook my head.

"That's Sean's ex."

"What?" I said a little too loudly, causing several heads to turn. I smiled brightly and held up a bottle of wine, indicating I'd be passing shortly. "Are you sure?" Nicole nodded. Just then, the cop turned and caught us staring at her. Thinking quickly, I waved her over to us.

"Would it be okay if I went around with some wine for the customers? You know, damage control…"

I could tell that she was about to say no, but then a sly smile crossed her lips. "Yes, that's not a bad idea, actually. Maybe it'll loosen some tongues a little. Good thinking!" She gave me and Nicole a toothy smile before moving on to another table.

"Do you still think it's her?" I whispered to Nicole.

"I'm pretty sure," she said, but this time with a hint of doubt.

"Well, don't forget that you're the one he was stalking a couple of months ago."

She sighed deeply. "Does it get any more awkward?" I was about to answer when the door opened. I groaned. Yeah, it certainly could get more awkward, and thanks for asking.

My parents zeroed in on me. "Vat the heck, Amalia?" my dad exclaimed. "Vat the cops doing heere again? Ve seeing all the flashing lights from da street as ve driving by." He looked at me with disappointment while my mom stood slightly behind him, her face pinched with worry.

"A lady collapsed in the parking lot and the ambulance came for her. The cops are just asking everyone for their account of what they saw." I shrugged and looked him straight in the eye. What? It was the truth. Okay, so I had that tingly gypsy feeling that there was *maybe* a bit more going on here, but in all honesty, that really was the truth, and according to them, there was no gypsy blood in our family.

I wasn't sure if it was my imagination, but I could have sworn my dad actually looked a little disappointed. It was just a fleeting and subtle change in his features.

"Oh, Amalia, *Bazd meg,*" he muttered, shaking his head. Yeah, yeah… And I knew what was coming.

"Listen, I'm not going to take accounting," I pre-empted, "so don't even start in on me about taking courses. Why don't you go over to one of the couches and have a seat? I'll bring you some wine."

To my surprise, they actually did as I had suggested. I'd thought that they would scurry out as fast as possible, but there was a look in my dad's eye that I recognized as my own. I watched as he looked about curiously, having taken a seat where he could see the entire room, and then he and my mom started to whisper. I brought them a glass of wine and then Nicole and I set about giving each of the customers a free glassful of Cheap red or Cheap white for the inconvenience of having to speak to the cops.

Laugh all you like, but I couldn't afford to be giving away glassfuls of more expensive wine. And in my defense, they both tasted good, and before the night was over, I even had requests for more. Nobody believed me when I told them it really was called Cheap.

By now, Officer Sean was working one side of the room while the female cop was finishing up in the section where we stood. She joined us for a moment, looking longingly at the wine bottles in the glass display case and the ones stocked behind the bar.

"Would you like water or coffee or something?" I offered.

She cleared her voice. "I'd love 'something', but water will have to do for now, thank you." I dashed back to the kitchen for some bottled water and was surprised to find the cop and Nicole having a conversation when I returned.

"I'm sorry about that night," the cop was saying. "Sean was helping me out, pretending to be my boyfriend. I had an ex there who refused to move on, so we were putting on a show for her benefit. She'd followed us out of the bar that night when we ran into you, so I had to make it look convincing. You threw a pretty good punch." She smiled brightly and I could see that Nicole was speechless. I jumped into the conversation.

"So, are you saying Sean really wasn't cheating on Nicole?"

She shrugged. "Not with me, he wasn't. Not my type. He's male." She smiled again and winked at Nicole, downed her water, and then moved on to another table.

"What the hell just happened here?" Nicole asked, her eyes as round as saucers.

"I have no clue. This is turning into an awfully strange evening. One thing is for sure, though: I think she likes you!" I winked at Nicole the way the cop had winked and then went to settle the bills of the customers who had given their statements and were waiting to leave.

Chapter Three

A couple of hours later, we were just about to close when a group of very handsome men wandered in and settled on the couches near the piano area, seemingly oblivious to the fact that we were closing. Only Nicole and I remained, since Beth had gone home as soon as she'd given her statement to the police. Five foxy men here to eat and drink? You guessed it…we stayed open.

Nicole walked over to take their orders while I admired them from afar. I couldn't help but gawk at one with slightly disheveled, wavy, light brown hair. I was always a sucker for the rugged looking ones, maybe as rebellion following my long years with the pretty boy, Hans. He caught me admiring him (in other words, undressing him with my eyes) and flashed me a brilliant smile. I immediately blushed and turned away.

Matt had been out of town on business for a couple of weeks, and my libido was in overdrive. Had the situation been reversed, however, I knew darn well that I wouldn't be happy if he was mentally undressing women. But I could not resist; I snuck another peak. Damn, he was still looking at me!

I bent down behind the bar counter, pretending to busy myself while I waited for Nicole to bring their orders. And that's when I saw it.

I leaned down further to pick it up, inspecting it in my hand. I had never been interested in drugs, but I knew a joint when I saw one. What was it doing here? None of us were smokers, and we definitely weren't tokers. Nora was a granny, Chloé's parents had been drug addicts and she was very passionately against it, and having known Nicole since the age of twelve, I knew she was against it too. That left one person. Beth. Was it hers, or had it fallen from a customer's pocket and somehow rolled back here? I knew I shouldn't jump to conclusions but what was I to think?

A male voice caused me to jump. "Hey, cool! I didn't know you were into that stuff," he said, clearly impressed.

"Billy, you scared the life out of me. You have to stop doing that. And this is not mine, and I'm not into this stuff," I said adamantly. He shrugged.

"Mind if I have it then?"

I handed it to him. "Be my guest. But what are you doing here? Anyway, I'm glad to see you."

Billy was a schizophrenic that I had met in recent months and who had saved my life when a snowmobile was barreling down at me and also when someone tried to kill me with an icicle. That's right; an icicle! He'd been off his meds at the time and falling deeper and deeper into a psychotic spiral, but he always had been kind to me, maybe because I kept feeding him like a stray cat. In any case, he was back on his meds now and managed to keep the voices that he heard at bay most days. I hadn't seen him in a couple of months but was happy to see him now.

"I came by to...uh...well...." he faltered, unsure how to continue. "Well, to ask for a job."

"Sure, we can find plenty for you to do. Whenever you want to work, just come by. Hey, how about right now?" I asked as Nicole arrived with the men's order. His eyes lit up.

"Sure, lady. What do you want me to do?"

"First, I want you to start calling me by my name, Amalia, or Mali if you prefer. Next, how about pouring five glasses of wine for Nicole to bring to that table while I go back to the kitchen to get a platter ready?" I indicated an imaginary line on the glass I was holding.

"Which wine?" We both looked at Nicole expectantly.

"Well, they left it up to me, so I asked what the occasion was, and it turns out that one of them was just dumped by his girlfriend, so how about a bottle of Bitch?" Billy's face turned deadly serious as he tried to find the Bitch. A smile crept slowly across his face, and then he burst out laughing. It was the first time I'd actually heard him laugh, and I was pleased by how far he'd apparently progressed since consenting to medical treatment.

"I get it!" he exclaimed. "All your bottles have funny names. I like that...Lady, Mali." I smiled over the grand title he'd bestowed upon me before heading back to the kitchen. The only other time he'd been inside this part of my bistro was when he'd saved me from a crazed attacker so he hadn't exactly had time to look around then and familiarize himself with the bistro.

Nicole supervised as Billy filled the glasses, then instructed him to place them on a tray so that it would be evenly balanced. Handing him a fresh dish towel, she suggested he wipe down the counter in case there were any little spills, and while he was doing that, she headed back to the table of men with the drinks.

A few moments later she joined me in the kitchen to collect the platter that I had prepared. Her eyes widened in surprise. "Hey, you got new cheese platters?"

I nodded, excited to share the news. "Yes, these arrived today. Aren't they gorgeous? I haven't had a chance to open and wash them all yet, otherwise I would have used them earlier." Being new to this business, I was still experimenting with ideas. I had ordered new wooden planks to be used as the serving platter and I was extremely pleased with the somewhat rustic look. I had lined up the salamis in the middle, a selection of cheeses in a ring around the meat and then an assortment of breads along the outside perimeter.

"Is that a new kind of salami, too?" Nicole licked her lips hungrily. Her excitement grew and my eyes shone. Clearly, it did not take much to excite us.

"It's called Alpen. It has just the right balance of salt, spices and smoke, and there's no greasy aftertaste. Here, try it!" I shoved a piece into her mouth and she chewed as though she hadn't eaten in days.

"Tastes great! Let me bring this out to the men and then I want leftovers. This is making me drool!"

I popped another piece of Alpen salami and a quick bite of fresh white Gouda cheese into my mouth and my eyes closed to savor the taste. This variety of Gouda was fairly mild and made in Canada. Some varieties were stronger but this one was one of my favorites. Nicole came back just as I finished the cheese. Caught in the act.

"I have something special for you," I told her. "But I don't want to leave Billy out there alone for too long. Save your appetite for half an hour and trust me; it'll be worth it." She nodded, though her mouth was again filled with Alpen salami.

Billy looked relieved when we returned. He had been standing by the bar as though glued to it and unsure what to do next. "Come with me, Billy, and I'll show you how to begin straightening up." He followed me about as I straightened chairs and tables and wiped down both and blew out candles. As we walked from table to table, I caught the curly-haired Adonis watching me from time to time and I soon began to blush. Our eyes locked before I tore mine away, again feeling guilty. I was with Matt, after all. My libido kicked me in response, not caring. Libido wanted Adonis.

"That's about all we can do right now, Billy," I said as we finished wiping down the last table. "Until the last of the customers are gone, we can't sweep out here, but you can take care of the kitchen if you like. Do you want to come by tomorrow night to give things a try on your own?" He readily agreed and asked if he could come at opening time. This was great news for me, since I wasn't sure if Beth would be up for another shift so soon after today's excitement. I'd much rather be overstaffed than short-handed. In any case, even if I was overstaffed, I cared about Billy and would have hired him regardless. I owed my life to him, twice, and it was the least I could do.

As Nicole went to settle the bill with the group of men, I watched in both fascination and horror as Adonis got up and walked in my direction. He smiled cautiously and I blushed in return as he sat on a stool at the bar. "Come here often?" he grinned, knowing full well he was delivering the cheesiest of lines. I had to laugh.

"Pretty much all the time, since I'm the owner," I replied. Although I'm not normally shy, this guy was making me sweat, and I was pretty sure he could tell. I could feel a bead form on my brow under my bangs. Please don't drip, I begged silently, as I felt it start to trickle.

"My name is Nathan." He offered his hand and I had no choice but to shake it with a sweaty paw.

"Amalia," I managed to squeak. To my relief, one of his buddies swooped down on us and clamped a hand on his shoulder. "Let's go, Nate."

He looked at me reluctantly, a smile still playing on his lips. "Nice to meet you," he said before getting up to join his friends. At the door, he gave me a lingering glance, as if he were mentally undressing me, and then he was gone. I exhaled the breath that I didn't realize I was holding. I wasn't sure what had just happened, and suddenly I wasn't quite sure how serious my feelings for Matt were, but Nathan had definitely had an effect on me.

"Let's eat," I suggested in response to Nicole's questioning gaze, as I was unprepared to answer any questions just yet. In the kitchen, I prepared some baked salami appetizers that I had made earlier, a new recipe that I'd been trying to perfect. Nicole was my willing guinea pig.

She carried the dish to a couch in the bistro while I chose a wine for us to taste-test. Yes, this was a difficult job, but someone had to do it, and I chose a cabernet sauvignon called Handsome Devil, all the while grinning to myself. As I poured the wine, Nicole couldn't help asking, "Did he ask you out?"

I shook my head. "No, but if his friend hadn't interrupted, I think he would have." I wouldn't meet her eyes because I knew that she knew me too well, and she would see my guilt, but also my curiosity, and more than likely my lust.

"So, how are things with you and Matt?" she asked cleverly.

"That's just it," I wailed. "Things between us are

fine! I'm sure we're fine. I mean, we get along great, and I love it when he's around, and I'm equally happy when he's not because I enjoy having time to concentrate on the bistro. But we go great together. Like salami and cheese. At least I think we do. I'm sure we do!"

So, why was I suddenly attracted to someone else?

"I have a feeling they'll all be back soon, if that curly-haired stud has anything to say about it," she speculated.

"That's what I'm afraid of," I groaned. And I was even more afraid of what I might do…

Baked Salami

- Salami of your choice, sliced to the thickness of your choice but not too thick (see below for suggestions)

- Herbed goat cheese or plain, spreadable cream cheese

- Dried or fresh dill weed or chives

Arrange the salami on a baking sheet or used but clean aluminum pie plate (I swear the pie plates cook everything to perfection!). Bake at 325 degrees for about 8-10 minutes, depending on the thinness, keeping a close eye on it so it doesn't burn. Another great idea is to bake in muffin tins to get a bowl effect.

Line plate with paper towel. Remove salami from heat, place on paper towels to blot and let cool. Once cool, top with about a teaspoon of your cheese and sprinkle with dill or another green herb of your choice (fresh chives or scallions are great too).

My suggestions for a good salami aren't very exclusive. Basically anything works well for this. In the States, I've even come across a salami called simply Salami and this worked well too. When I tried this recipe with something a bit spicy, like a nice Mexican or Mustard Seed Salami, it kicked it up a notch.

You can also bake pepperoni. To do it the really easy way, place a sheet of paper towel on a plate and place as many pepperoni rounds as you can on it. Then microwave for about 45 seconds and check them. If they need a bit more time, another 15 to 20 seconds should be all it takes for some yummy pepperoni chips. As microwave times vary, test a few at a time as this one is a bit tricky to master. I, personally, haven't mastered it yet, but I've seen great results by those who have.

Chapter Four

I locked the doors as Nicole left and finished tidying up, then went upstairs to my living quarters. I took my thyroid pill with a tall glass of water then sank down gratefully on the couch and snuggled my cat, Hummer, allowing his loud rumbling purrs to soothe my frazzled nerves.

It had been a long and eventful day. With my Hashimoto's hypothyroid condition, I was already battling energy issues on a daily basis. Eventful days took their toll even if my condition was fairly stable. I was just dozing off when I felt the cat batting at my nose with a paw. For him, it was play time. I shook his paw, gave his nose a kiss and shuffled off to my room to crash for a few hours.

I awoke around ten the next morning, wonderfully refreshed. Checking my phone, I was pleased to find a text from Matt, but was sad when I read it.

"I'll be gone for another week," Matt's text indicated with a sad face emoji. We seldom spoke, mainly because I hated talking on the phone but also because it was just easier via text with both of our busy schedules.

"Okay, stay safe," I wrote back. Matt, an ex-cop, now had his own private eye and security guard company. These days, he normally busied himself with running the place and scheduling jobs and personnel, but from time to time, some of his most lucrative clients requested him specifically. He was on such a job at the moment, which had taken him to southern Florida on a fact gathering mission.

Neither of us wrote that we loved each other since we hadn't gotten to that stage yet. Although we'd been together for nearly four months, the topic just hadn't come up and I don't think either of us was in a hurry to go there, not to mention that we had some fairly long periods of time where we didn't see each other. Things were great the way they were, and we both knew we cared for each other in some fashion, and until 'Adonis' had come along, I hadn't had eyes (or loins) for anyone else.

Not wanting to think about it, I leaped out of bed and got ready to face the day.

I had just finished pre-slicing the cheeses and salamis when Chloé and Billy arrived almost simultaneously. She gave me a questioning glance, knowing who Billy was, but not why he was here. I greeted them both warmly. Billy's eyes shone as his gaze landed on her. He'd had a little crush on her, I suspected, having seen her from afar a number of times.

"Come inside, you guys, and have a seat on one of

the couches. Once Nora and my mom are here, we'll have a little group meeting. Billy's going to be helping us from time to time. I haven't heard from Beth yet, but I don't think…" I broke off as she entered the room.

"I'm here," she announced with a bright smile. She seemed well, as though nothing out of the ordinary had happened the day before.

"Then we'll just wait for Mum. Beth, this is Billy, a friend of mine who saved my life a couple of times, literally. He'll be helping us." They shook hands and Billy glanced from Beth to Chloé and back, as though trying to decide what he'd like for dessert. Clearly, he was taken with both and upon closer inspection, other than their height difference and hair styles, they looked strikingly similar with their ebony hair and olive complexions. Chloé had straightened her curly hair today, so the resemblance was even more striking between the two young ladies who had become fast friends. After a few moments of bobbing his head back and forth, his gaze settled on Beth, and I could tell that he had made a choice.

"Beth, I'll be there shortly to talk about what happened yesterday," I said, in other words, warning her not to discuss it yet. She nodded and headed into the bistro with the other two. I finished preparing a little snack for them while we waited for my mother to arrive.

Yes, my mother! Anyu, in Hungarian. The better half of the Aliens. A few weeks back, I had placed a suggestion box near the bar in the bistro, and an over-whelming number of requests to include my mom's schnitzel permanently on the menu had been regis-tered. A few times in the past, when I was injured, or when we were short staffed at the bistro, my mom had donned her apron and prepared her now-famous specialty. Amazed by the number of people willing to clog their arteries, I gave in and asked Mum if she'd like to come in once a week, and although she found a full shift to be quite tiring, she had jumped at the chance.

Mum arrived slightly out of breath due to the extra pounds she carried; nevertheless she was ready for business proudly sporting one of our promo-tional t-shirts that declared, "Ask me about my Frisky Beaver." God help me!

A hug and kiss later, with her light brown whiskers gently grazing my cheek, she followed me to join the others. Since Nicole and Nora had the night off, I proceeded with the details of yesterday's events, which Billy and Chloé had not yet heard about.

Billy looked worried for a moment then shrugged and went back to admiring both girls, but mainly Beth. Everyone seemed satisfied that the unfortu-nate woman had died of natural causes rather than a murder, and while they were sad, they didn't seem overly concerned. Even Beth, who had been quite shaken the day before, appeared to be good as new.

"This probably means we'll be super busy today," Chloé said, ever the optimist. "Such things draw curiosity seekers. As a matter of fact, there are a couple of people already sitting on the veranda."

Damn it! I had meant to put away the patio furniture but after the events of the past twenty-four hours, I'd totally forgotten. "Billy, at the end of each evening, would you to put away the patio furniture, please?"

"Sure, I can do that, Mali." He grinned, obviously pleased by the novelty of calling me by my first name. Then we all helped to light the candles while my mum retreated to the kitchen to prepare the schnitzel. Hearing a commotion on the porch, I peered outside to see a crowd forming and decided to open a bit early.

"I'd like to reserve the patio for next Friday at five, please," one lady said as she sailed inside. Another couple, hot on her heels, piped up, "And we'd like the following afternoon, please."

I pasted a polite smile onto my face, which likely was more of a grimace, as I half-heartedly scratched their names into my reservation book. I scribbled myself a reminder note to tell Billy not to bother moving the chairs, after all.

Chloé and Beth attended to the couples inside, Billy stood glued to the bar and I ventured out to check on the customers occupying my patio chairs. To my surprise, a bony butt flapping in the air was what greeted my eyes. "Is everything okay?" I asked.

"Oh, Greg, get up," a blonde woman chided. A tall, lanky man got to his feet and grinned sheepishly.

"Sorry, I thought I lost something here last night but

I must be mistaken," he said as he sat on a patio chair.

He looked familiar but I couldn't quite place him. "Would you like to leave your name and number and what you lost, in case it turns up?" I offered.

"No, it's nothing important," he assured me before changing the subject. "Could you bring us two glasses of white wine, please? We may order some food later, but the wine will do for now."

I nodded and turned to go back inside but stopped in my tracks when two police cruisers pulled into the parking lot. "What now?" I muttered under my breath as I watched the female officer from the day before exit a vehicle. She waved in my direction but didn't approach. Four officers in total began to inspect the parking lot, inch by inch. I turned to re-assure the couple on the patio that it likely had to do with an unfortunate death that had occurred here at the bistro the previous day.

The lanky man nodded. "Yes, we were here yesterday when it happened." The blonde next to him nodded absently as she watched the cops. "I thought that the police had determined that it was a natural death."

I shrugged. "Did you know the woman who died?" I asked straight out.

The man shook his head. "Blanche? No, we didn't know her." I stared at him in confusion but he offered nothing further, his concentration focused on the investigation going on right in front of his eyes.

He claimed not to know the woman, however he'd just referred to her by her name.

I returned with the wine, two glasses of My Secret. He had refused to tell me what he'd been looking for, they had been here yesterday, and they obviously knew Blanche, and probably Milton, too. Plus, I just recalled that they were the couple that tried to slink out of the bistro before being questioned by the police. In my eyes, they had both just became suspects.

"Here you are, Mr. and Mrs…."

"Gregson," the blonde replied, her concentration still on the cops. That meant her husband's name was Greg Gregson? I did a mental head slap.

The female cop made her way over to me and smiled before getting to the point. "We don't have all the results yet, but we did get confirmation that the cause of death is not evident at this time."

"What exactly does that mean?" I asked as I drew her away from the eavesdropping couple. "Does it mean that she was murdered?"

Officer Lynette looked at my hand, which was still on her arm. "Sorry," I explained, "but I think the couple on the patio knew her, and I know that they were here yesterday. I didn't want them to overhear us talking."

She casually glanced their way. "You didn't happen to catch a name, did you?"

"Greg Gregson," I replied. "And they tried to sneak out of the bistro before being questioned yesterday."

"Well done! I hear that you've gotten involved with cases in the past, but I think it would be best if you'd leave this to us. I'll check them out."

I nodded nervously. "Trust me; I have no interest in getting involved." Just then, my pseudo-aneurism twitched, making the entire left side of my face contort ever so slightly and just for a second. Officer Lynette looked at me more closely, and I smiled sweetly and let her think that she was seeing things.

I returned inside and asked Beth to check on the Gregsons while I lent my mother a hand in the kitchen. She was making schnitzel like a mad woman and complaining about the heat. Frying was definitely hot work, so I turned on a fan then pitched in to help.

Several minutes later, Beth poked her head inside the kitchen and requested a schnitzel platter. I had already pre-plated a number of servings as the schnitzels had come out of the oil, anticipating that the orders would start coming in. As she took the platter, I could see her hands shake slightly.

"Are you okay? You're shaking!" I observed with concern.

"I guess I just didn't eat much today," she replied, turning to go.

"Who is this for, anyway?"

"The couple on the patio," she replied. I studied her for a moment then took the platter from her and brought it out to the patio myself. To my surprise, a different couple was now seated there, the Gregsons apparently having left already. I noticed that the cops were still roaming around the lot and wondered idly if that could be what had Beth so preoccupied.

When I returned to the kitchen, Beth was still

there. "Why don't you go out back for some fresh air?" I suggested. She nodded in agreement.

She returned about ten minutes later, looking as good as new, and went back to her duties.

My mom sniffed at the cloud of smoke that had followed her inside and asked in Hungarian, "What the hell is she smoking?"

I remembered the joint that I had found and made a mental note to keep my eyes open.

Chapter Five

A few uneventful days passed, for which I was extremely thankful. Although we'd exchanged several texts and even talked a couple of times, Matt was still away so I was free to lie around and be lazy. After lounging in bed for several hours on Wednesday morning, drinking coffee and watching cooking shows with Hummer, I finally made myself presentable. My Wednesday cheese and salami order would be arriving in a couple of hours but first I had to make a trip to the bakery for fresh bread.

Ready to leave, I swung open the door and was greeted by a fist to my nose. My father swung around in horror, apologizing profusely. He'd been looking out over the parking lot while in the midst of lifting his hand to knock on my door and had instead rapped sharply on my poor little nose.

I waved him inside then checked my nose for blood while he laughed sheepishly and then apologized again. Once I ascertained that all was well, I turned my gaze toward him. "What's going on?" I could tell that something was on his mind, especially since he kept looking out the window toward the parking lot. He answered in Hungarian, too excited to attempt English.

"Did you hear the news?" he asked, his eyes shining. "The lady from your parking lot did *not* die of natural causes." He waited for a reaction. I wasn't surprised, however, since the police had returned a couple of times to look around. He continued to pace about, bobbing upon his bad knee. "They say it might be poison." I waited for him to lecture me and badger me to become an accountant but was surprised to simply find him looking at me expectantly.

"How do you know all this, Dad?" I asked, curiosity getting the better of me.

"Mr. Leonardo told me," he replied. My parents did not yet know about my feud with Leonardo. "I was picking up a pizza there and we started talking. He's a nice man."

I bit my tongue to prevent myself from having an outburst. Nice man? This nice man threw bats of pepperoni at me and hated me simply because I was the only other eatery in town. We had almost been friendly a few months back, but when my good friend Nora had broken up with him after a brief fling, he found out she knew me and decided to blame me for the breakup. Anything he could blame me for, he did. To make matters worse, he refused to sell me pizza, and I love pizza. I huffed at the memory before turning my attention back to my father. Or was he now my pizza connection?

"Does he know you're my father?" I couldn't quite keep the sharp edge out of my tone.

He thought for a moment. "I don't think that came up. We were just talking about the town of Robin and I mentioned that we had moved here not long ago, and then he mentioned that some police were in his restaurant and he overheard them talking about the lady. He did say that you can't seem to keep yourself out of trouble, though. Do you know the man? He seemed to think it was quite funny, but before I could ask him anything else, some other people entered."

"Yes, you could say we know each other. Mr. Leonardo does not like me because he sees me as competition. So, if you want to be able to buy pizza from him, don't tell him you know me. You'll be banished forever."

He shook his head in disbelief, repeating my name over and over in that special, disappointed way he has. I shrugged. I was used to it. "How do you keep getting involved in things like this?" he asked.

"I'm not involved," I finally shouted, unable to contain my agitation any longer. "They sat on my patio then she died when she was crossing the parking lot. This has nothing to do with me!"

"I know where he lives," my dad said softly. I thought I imagined it and gaped at him for a moment.

"How do you know where he lives? And why are you telling me this?" My aneurism twitched in double time.

"The pizza man told me. The man whose wife died is very well known—everyone knows where he lives. I thought that maybe you'd like to go for a drive and show me the neighborhood." Was this man, my father, somehow encouraging me to snoop around? Was he implying he would snoop with me? There it was. That sparkle that I thought I had seen the day of the *incident*. Where was this sudden curiosity coming from? Incredulous, I stared at him, unable to form words. "Vat?" he asked innocently. "Ve going for drive now?" His sudden change to English flustered me. I looked at my watch.

"I have exactly one hour to spare, and then I have to visit the Rideau Bakery to buy my breads. Okay, let's go." I grabbed my keys and purse before he could change the mind that he had clearly lost.

We drove toward the Ottawa River then turned left, meandering along the street and admiring the eclectic mix of old cottages and remodeled mansions. A number of them were in transition in this area that was being bought up by the more affluent residents of Ottawa who wanted waterfront property that was still close to the city.

"Slower," my dad barked, his eyes searching the house numbers. "I think we're getting close; the house should be just ahead." I pulled over to let a black car that was right on my tail sail past then resumed at a crawl. Just ahead, I could see the portly shape of an older man waddling along the road then stop to talk to a lady walking her dog. Excited and alert, I sat up straight and slammed on the brakes.

"That's him, Dad!" Thoughts raced through my head. Should I stop and talk to him? Offer him a ride? I crawled along at a snail's pace. Before I could formulate a plan, the car that had passed us just moments ago came hurtling back toward me, then suddenly swerved. Milton sailed into the ditch at the side of the road, and as I braked and squeezed my eyes closed, waiting for impact, I heard the furious barking of the dog and then the squeal of tires.

Chapter Six

No impact came. Just the sound of ragged breathing filled the car, along with a hint of garlic.

And all I wanted to do today was buy bread! That was all I could think of before the image of Milton diving into the ditch replayed in my head. Opening my eyes, I saw the dog lady face down on the road. I quickly pulled over and turned off the ignition. My dad looked at me in confusion and then we both bolted from the car. With his bad leg, he bobbed as quickly as he could to catch up to me.

The tiny dog snarled with the fury that one would expect from a dragon. As I approached, I slowed so as not to further alarm it. To my relief, the lady moaned. That was good. One must be alive to moan.

"Shut up, Beast," she barked at her dog. "You're giving me a headache. You there, Missy, call an ambulance, would you?" She turned her beady eyes on me before opening her mouth and bellowing, "Milton, where the hell are you? This is all your fault, and I'm going to sue your ugly, fat ass!"

"I'll get my cell phone," I said as my dad went to check the ditch. I ran back to the car for my phone, called for an ambulance and assured the dispatcher that the lady was alive but likely had a broken bone or two. I then joined my dad and we both dragged Milton from the ditch, slipping along the grassy slope from the burden of his weight. He reached the road, sputtering something between not quite a thank you and a complaint about our rough handling before his eyes landed on me.

He held a meaty paw up to the woman still screeching at him as he regarded me oddly, nostrils flaring. He finally spoke: "You," he said flatly. "What are you doing here? Are you the one that's been after me? Did you kill my wife?" This last question boomed like thunder and I jumped. I may even have peed a little.

"I'll kill you myself, you miserable coot," the lady on the ground shrilled furiously. "You're a rotten neighbor. Nothing but trouble around here, and I'm sure you're involved. If this woman was after you, you fat idiot, then she wouldn't be standing here trying to help us. Now come over here and help me up." Milton blinked in surprise then turned on her.

"You're one to talk, you old battleax, with your whiny dog. Too bad that car didn't hit your damned dog, too. It would have been a favor to society!"

"Are you saying that that car was aiming for *me*? I'm sure the driver was after you, you old fart!" She was still spewing obscenities as my dad and I helped her to her feet. Milton refused to help and stood glaring at us all.

She howled furiously at him. "You're going to pay for my broken leg, and my pain and suffering. Mark my words!"

"How is it my fault? I'm a victim just as you are," he sputtered, glaring at me again as though I was somehow responsible. "Weren't you about to tell me what you're doing here?" he demanded, his glare intensifying.

"I was just showing my father the area—he's new to town. You're lucky we came along when we did, otherwise you might both be dead." He did not need to know that the real reason we were in the area was to figure out where he lived.

"This man has as many enemies as he has dollars," the older lady rasped, glaring at him. "And he's as miserable as they come. I wouldn't mind killing him myself!"

He returned her haughty stare. "I wouldn't be surprised if someone decided to do something about you and your yapping dog," he said as we heard the ambulance shriek from a distance.

"Did either of you get a look at the person driving the car?" I asked to disarm their fury.

"She had long blonde hair, that's all I could tell," the woman muttered, her face grimacing in pain now that her anger and adrenaline were wearing off.

"I didn't see anything," Milton said. "Once I saw the front of the car heading toward us, I jumped as far as I could. I may not be as spry as I was in my younger days," he boasted, "but I can still move pretty fast when I have to." He actually looked proud of his flying leap into the ditch.

"Well, one thing I can't accuse you of is being a gentleman. You left me there to fend for myself," the older lady shrilled, her wail blending in with the sound of the ambulance that was now upon us. Luckily, we were now spared from their verbal tennis match.

The paramedics leaped out of the ambulance and walked towards us quickly but calmly, seeing that the lady was now standing and that there no longer appeared to be a sense of urgency. My eyes widened in dismay as I noted the light brown, curly hair and muscled torso. Then those magnificent blue eyes shifted toward me, blazing in recognition. My loins blazed in return and I felt one of those annoying and immediate pangs of guilt. I firmly reminded my loins about Matt before smiling tentatively at Nathan, the stud from the bistro.

They had just loaded the woman into the back of the ambulance when a police car arrived on the scene. Nathan gave me a dazzling smile and a wave before leaving us with the police. I was left with the distinct feeling that I'd be seeing him again soon.

My dad, Milton, and I all gave accounts of the hit and run and gave our contact information before being given the okay to proceed with our day. By now, Milton had calmed down considerably and I felt a pang of sympathy as I studied his sagging features.

This was a man that obviously ate well and gave little concern for his physique. I wondered why he was out walking as it seemed out of character considering what little I knew of him. "Can we give you a lift, sir?" I offered.

His sudden mirth surprised me. "You want to give me a lift up my own driveway? I live right here." He cocked his head to indicate the house we were standing in front of but which we really hadn't had a chance to notice with all the excitement. I gawked at the long driveway leading to the sprawling home and the immaculately manicured lawn.

"Well, it looks like a pretty long driveway," I joked, and surprisingly he laughed.

"One of the longest around here, in fact…" He beamed proudly then marched over to my car and hopped into the front passenger seat, forcing my dad to maneuver himself into the back seat. I hurried to join them and then drove the man within a few feet of his front door.

"Thank you," he said, obviously not used to conveying gratitude. He heaved himself out of my old Mazda. Before he could close the door, I spoke quickly.

"My condolences, sir, about your wife. She always seemed like a nice lady when I saw her at the Whine and Cheese. Will you be okay here by yourself?"

He gave me that flat, mirthless look that seemed to be his signature. "I'm not alone. My housekeeper and my cook are inside, and my gardener is around here somewhere. And if he had been doing what he was supposed to be doing, then he would have seen Mrs. Knuedle and her dog taking a crap on my lawn, and I wouldn't have had to go down there to give her a piece of my mind!" He stomped away as I resisted the urge to laugh at the image of the old lady taking a crap on the lawn, even though I was pretty sure he was referring to the dog.

"So, who do you think might be after you?" I called out to his retreating backside, earning a glare from my dad who clearly wanted this to end so that he could return home.

To my surprise, the fat man turned to look at me, this time without disdain, and shrugged. "Many of these people had investments through my firm, and most of them lost money when the market went south. Some blame me personally."

I followed the line of his gaze to the house across the street where I saw someone standing in front of the window. The person realized that we were looking at him and disappeared quickly behind the curtains. I felt the hairs rise on the back of my neck, though I couldn't explain why.

"Where does Mrs. Knuedle live?" I asked.

"The lady dragon lives right there, and I have to listen to her damn dog day and night. I have half a mind to… Never mind. But if Blanche were still alive, she'd be able to tell you more, because she knew everyone, including the druggies down the street. Blanche was kind to everyone."

He suddenly choked up and shifted his gaze to

the ground, blinking furiously and uttering a single sob. Regaining his composure, he looked at me with heavy eyes. "You'd better take your father home, Miss. He's not looking well." With that, he turned on his heel and went through his front door.

Chapter Seven

I glanced at my dad and noticed that Milton was right.

"Do you want to see the rest of the neighborhood?" I offered sweetly, unable to resist having a little fun at his expense. After all, this was his fault. He had dragged me here when I was determined to stay out of another mystery. I'm pretty sure I was, anyway. With a feeble voice he asked me to take him back to my place.

Once we were home, I gave Nicole a call to ask if she could make a trip to the bakery for me for breads, since I wouldn't be able to make it back in time for opening. Then I settled my father on a couch with a small glass of Rough Day. He had been so excited earlier but clearly regretted his involvement now. I studied him silently, suddenly aware of how he'd aged in recent years. Although I joke about how different my parents are and call them Aliens, I do love them dearly, and it saddened me to see him shaken. The sentimental moment didn't last.

"Vat the heck, Amalia?" he suddenly boomed.

"Vat?" I shrieked in return, taken off guard.

"Something always happens when you're around." He switched to rapid-fire Hungarian. Hungarian is already a rather angry sounding language and now he was clearly pissed off. "We were just going for a drive and then someone almost gets killed. What is wrong with you that these things keep happening?"

"Stop right there," I bellowed right back, but in English since I'm incapable of arguing in Hungarian. "I'm not to blame here! It was your idea to go there. How can this hit and run possibly be blamed on me? And furthermore, why in the world would you even suggest that we go there? What were you thinking?"

I'd blurted it out and put the blame where it belonged, right in his pudgy lap. Although I could see that he was angry at my outburst, he sat solemnly, drinking his wine in silence. I was starting to think he wouldn't even answer me.

"I guess I was just curious, and when Mr. Leonardo mentioned where Milton lived, I thought we might take a look...together. Knowing you, you will be involved in this anyway, so this way, I thought I could keep you safe. I was wrong. I'm too old to keep you safe." He shrugged his shoulders and instantly looked ten years older, bringing tears to my eyes.

"*Bazd meg,*" I muttered under my breath as I refilled his glass with more liquid courage. "Drink up, Dad, you'll be fine. Trust me, you get used to it after a while and learn to just go with it. Now that Milton's wife officially was declared poisoned, you may be right that I'm going to try to look into this. Once again, the bistro's reputation will be at stake, and I can't risk losing everything."

"Why vud it affecting yore bistro?" he asked in English.

"They ate at my bistro and then she collapsed in my parking lot. Everyone's going to think it was something in my food!" I could barely keep the whine out of my voice and fought hard not to let him see how upset I truly was. Unfortunately for me, he can be quite shrewd at times.

"Vare is Mutt?" he asked out of the blue.

"He's out of town on a case. Why?"

"He used to be cop, so maybe he can get information for you."

Although Matt probably could get information from cops, so far he hadn't helped me very much with past cases. "I'll ask him, but he won't be home for a few more days, and I don't want to worry him while he's out of town. Come on, I'll drive you home in your car then I'll walk back. I don't think you should drive right now." I eyed the half bottle of wine he'd sucked back, quite impressed. I didn't think he had it in him.

Chapter Eight

I brought my dad home then hiked the mile or so back to the bistro, arriving in time to help Nicole unload the Rideau Bakery breads from her car. Rushing to prepare everything in time to open, we chopped as quickly as we could but jumped as the back door burst open. Nora waltzed inside, her breasts high and proud in what was obviously a push-up bra. Nicole and I exchanged a glance. Nora had last sported a push-up when she'd left her husband and taken up with my nemesis, Mr. Leonardo.

"Hello, ladies; it's good to be back! I've missed you both." She gave us both a busty hug then rolled up her sleeves. "What can I do to help? It looks like we're a bit behind."

"You could chop the veggies for salads." I thrust several heads of lettuce her way. We hadn't seen her in a while since she'd been spending more time with her husband Craig. After they'd reunited she seemed focused on salvaging the marriage, so the reappearance of the push-up bra was a concern.

"Is everything okay?" Nicole probed as we exchanged another glance.

"Why wouldn't it be? What's new around here? Has anything interesting happened?" My guilty thoughts turned briefly to Nathan, and for some reason, I pictured him in sexy boxers.

"To be honest, Nora, that bra is a symbol of your Leonardo days," Nicole blurted out. A smile tugged at the edges of Nora's lips as she softly repeated his name. Then she glared at us.

"Don't read too much into things," she snapped, which was totally out of character. We shrugged and worked in silence for a while.

"There's been another murder," I said, remembering that she hadn't been around when it had occurred and that it would probably be news to her.

Nora's eyes widened. She had been living with me during her temporary break-up when a body was found inside my garage, and she had helped with the investigation. "Isn't that exciting?"

I recapped the events for her then added the latest news.

"It seems that the victim was poisoned. Since her last meal was here at the bistro, it doesn't look good for me. I've had police combing the parking lot as well as the bistro and even my living quarters upstairs. Obviously, they didn't find any poison here, so I'm thankful that the murderer did not plant fake evidence here to frame me. When word gets out though, it's bound to affect business. I mean, I'm sure people won't be anxious to eat here." I also outlined the events earlier that day, when Milton had been the target of a hit and run driver.

"How did you find out about the poison?" Nora asked when I'd finished recounting the events.

"Apparently, Leonardo overheard the cops discussing the case and shared the information with my dad, who just happened to be there at the time." Call it my latent gypsy senses, but I was definitely picking up a weird vibe from Nora.

"Perhaps I should pay him a visit," she suggested.

"No!" Nicole and I both shouted, making Nora jump.

"We need all the information we can get. Leave it to me." Then she and her boobs sashayed into the bistro to begin lighting candles. Her posture had sex written all over it, and not the married kind of sex, either.

A couple of hours later, I retreated to my private little garden in the backyard. Once I had realized my patio would be booked for dinners and resigned myself to that fact, I had moved the Oleanders to the back to make way for another chair in the front. Now, with tears streaming down my face, I sat in my peaceful spot and took comfort in admiring the Lily of the Valley flowers and Foxgloves that surrounded the two patio chairs I had set up in the back for the staff to take breaks.

I swiped angrily at the tears that left a wet trail down my cheek and slid down my neck. I knew that once the word of the poisoning got out, it wouldn't be good for business, but I hoped my regular customers would remain loyal. I certainly didn't think word would get out this fast, as only a handful of customers dared to cross my threshold today. Since I had opened just over five months earlier, this was the first day that we'd barely had a customer, and I feared it wouldn't be the last. My business had never been affected before, but obviously this was different since poison could be slipped into food and drinks so easily. Of course, there was nothing to indicate she'd consumed the poison at the bistro, but that didn't stop speculation.

I felt a hand pat my shoulder as I wiped away the last of the tears. I did not make an attractive damsel in distress.

"This will blow over," Nora said as she took a seat on the chair next to me. "Listen, since you don't need me today, I'm going to leave now. I'll be a lot more help to you if I pay Leo a visit and get some information."

I sighed knowing I could not refuse her offer even though it disgusted me to the core. I had left a message for Officer Lynette earlier, asking for information, but I'd received no return call. "What's his last name, anyway? You call him Leo, while most people call him Mr. Leonardo, but I know Leonardo is his first name. I can't recall if I ever heard his last name."

"I never thought to ask," she confessed. "We didn't spend much time talking." She winked and patted me on the shoulder again and took her leave as I gagged.

I let out a big, unhappy sigh that turned into a shriek when I felt another skeletal hand on my shoulder. Beth plunked her skinny frame down on the chair next to me and lit up what I hoped and thought was only a cigarette.

"I didn't mean to scare you," she said around a mouthful of smoke, and then turned her head to blow it away from me, knowing that I was allergic to tobacco. Fascinated, I watched her in silence as she blew smoke rings.

"That blond streak in your hair looks cute," I complimented her as the waning sun glinted off the blond strand.

"I do that every now and then," she muttered, raising the cigarette to her lips again. I wasn't sure if I imagined it but her hand seemed to shake slightly. I waited quietly and continued to watch her smoke.

"Are you upset about something?" I finally asked.

"Actually, I am. About the poison…" I was uncertain where she was going with this line of thought. "Nicole says that you'll get to the bottom of this. She told me that you've done some sleuthing in the past. I had no idea, Mali. Do you think I might help? I mean, since I'm the one who served the deceased, I'm worried that I'll be implicated."

As I reached over and patted her hand, an idea percolated in the dark corners of my brain. "I'm sure you can help. Give me a day or two to come up with a plan."

She flashed me a smile. "Thank you, Mali. Do you mind if I go now? There really aren't many customers. I'm pretty sure that you and Nicole and Billy can manage."

I nodded my approval then said, "Call me tomorrow about the work schedule for the rest of the week." I had another little cry then squared my shoulders and marched back inside the bistro. Once inside, I said to Billy, "Open a bottle of Troublemaker, and also a bottle of Murder on my Mind, and pour everyone who's here a free glass of wine to thank them for their patronage. Tell them to spread the word, too. I'll be upstairs. I've got some planning to do." I stopped long enough to pour myself a large glass of red and chugged half of it before topping it up again. Billy shuffled off to serve the wine.

As this was his first time actually serving customers, I lingered for a moment to ensure that he was okay. Then I stomped upstairs, giving Nicole a quick wave from across the room and motioning to her where I was going. She read me like an open book.

Lemon Cheesecake Squares

Well, that chapter was a bit of a downer. But when life hands me lemons, I like to make something yummy with them. I can't take the credit for this next recipe as it's something I came across on Pinterest. What I did, however, is combine the elements from different (but similar) recipes and, of course, add my own touch. Any way you look at it, it's deliciously simple.

- 2 (8 ounces each) bars of cream cheese (I use light)

- 2 lemons

- 1 egg, with the yolk and egg white separated

- 2 small packages of Pillsbury crescent roll dough (the regular, original size, 235g)

- ½ cup white granulated sugar

- 1 teaspoon almond extract or vanilla extract

- 2 cups shredded, unsweetened coconut flakes

- 2-4 tablespoons granulated sugar

- Lemon zest (from your two lemons)

Heat oven to 350 degrees F (175 C).

Meanwhile, take a small baking dish and spray with cooking spray or coat with a thin film of butter or margarine (I used a 9-inch by almost 9-inch dish but you can probably go a bit larger).

Using one can of the crescent roll dough, press onto the bottom of your greased baking dish, making sure dough reaches all edges.

Next, zest both lemons. Use half of zest and combine with the juice from both lemons, cream cheese, sugar, egg white and almond extract. Mix with electric mixer until smooth then spread over crescent roll dough in your pan. Sprinkle coconut overtop.

Using second can of dough, place dough evenly over the filling, again making sure it reaches all edges. Brush the top with the egg yolk then sprinkle the rest of your lemon zest over the top. Last, but not least, sprinkle 2 to 4 tablespoons of granulated sugar overtop (I like to use four).

Bake for about 30-40 minutes or until top is golden. Let cool for 20-30 minutes before cutting into squares, then refrigerate for about an hour, until well chilled. When ready, feel free to sprinkle with a thin dusting of icing sugar (what can I say, I love sugar. Plus, it looks so pretty).

Note: this must cool in the fridge for a good hour or more to properly set.

Chapter Nine

Knowing Matt would eventually find out, I texted him an overview of the details and advised him that I intended to track down leads. Then I sat back and waited. Within minutes my phone broke out in an Eminem song, my ringtone.

I hadn't even said hello yet but I could hear Matt already lecturing me. "Are you crazy? How many times have I almost lost you? Just let the cops do their job. Please! They might not be able to tell you much, but I'm sure they're working around the clock."

Despite my boiling blood, I replied calmly. He should know by now that I didn't respond well to being told what to do. What was he thinking? "Matt, I had a total of five couples at the bistro today," I stated simply. He knew how many tables my bistro held and that the turnover during the course of the evening was at least three or four times. "The money I made didn't even cover salaries for today. I have to get this cleared up, pronto, or there will be no bistro. If there's no bistro, then there is no house since the profits are what pays my mortgage. You know very well that the police are not working around the clock on this, and quite honestly, the thought of being homeless and having to live with my mother and father turns my stomach."

I was answered with silence as the impact of my words registered. "I'm sorry," he finally said, barely above a whisper. Maybe he was scared senseless at the thought of me having to move in with him if I lost the house. That would certainly send the relationship into new territory that I didn't think either of us was ready to explore.

"Let me get in touch with Ricky. I'll ask him to make some calls and help you in any way that he can. I should be back in a few more days." Ricky worked for Matt and they had been partners when they were both cops. More than once, Ricky had helped out. He was a kind and loyal friend, not to mention an excellent private investigator. And the fact that Matt was even offering to help was epic. With a promise to check in on me the next day, we hung up.

I heard a tap on the door that led from the bistro up to my kitchen, and then Nora poked her silver head inside, grinning from ear to ear. I started to grin back but my smile froze as I took note of her disheveled hair and rumpled clothing. She hadn't…had she? I dared not ask as I was not ready to hear the answer. I grabbed a wine glass for her and filled it to the brim before topping mine up again. I couldn't listen to any of this sober since I was still busy moping.

Nora sank onto the couch next to me and sighed happily as she guzzled her wine, smacking her lips after each sip. "I did miss Leo," she said softly, mostly to herself. Noting the use of the past tense, I gagged again and promptly changed the subject.

"Did you find out anything useful?"

She nodded, her eyes shining with excitement. "Oh, yes! It's definitely a case of poisoning, but they haven't determined which one yet. There seems to be something unusual about it, and from what Leo's overheard, it may be more than one kind of poison, and not the usual ones, so they're doing additional testing. She also had some medical conditions, so that, combined with the poisons, might be what caused such a sudden death, unless she'd been ingesting the poisons for some time. Once they have the lab work completed, they'll know more."

I leaned forward. "What were the other medical conditions?"

"Apparently, she'd had a heart condition from a young age, an electrolyte imbalance and low blood pressure, too, and she was diabetic, and she was on antibiotics for some type of infection. So with all that combined, her immune system was probably compromised. And that's not all…" She leaned closer to me and lowered her voice for no apparent reason. "She had needle marks."

She sat back, a smug look on her face, and downed the rest of her wine.

I gnawed at my lip, deep in thought. "Needle

marks? So you're suggesting that the poison was injected? Then I should be in the clear, because it wouldn't have been anything in the food…"

"I don't know about that, Mali. The first thing I thought of when I heard about needle marks was drugs, or maybe they were from the insulin injections, or possibly from bloodwork done to isolate the bacteria causing the infection. Do you think she looked like a drug user?"

"Not really. But Milton did mention that they had drug dealers living in the neighborhood. Now this is interesting, isn't it? Well done, Nora!"

She beamed with pride and stuck out her chest a bit more. "I have more news too," she teased, holding out her wine glass for a refill. I ran to the kitchen, topped it up and returned with the rest of the bottle just in case.

Nora was squirming on the couch with excitement. "Now don't get mad…"

I immediately began to get mad. "For God's sake, what have you done?"

"Nothing yet. But I'm thinking about going under cover."

Not liking the direction this conversation was taking, I nodded for her to continue.

"Leo is short-staffed this week, so he asked me if I wanted to work a few evenings. Naturally, I said yes, because since the cops are always in there, I'll be able to get more information."

I could feel the wine curdling in my belly. "What

exactly will you tell Craig?" I finally asked. No doubt her husband would be less than thrilled with this development. She avoided my gaze.

"I'll figure out something, Mali. Don't worry. For the next couple of evenings he'll think I'm here, anyway. I think I'm having a mid-life crisis," she confessed.

Mid-life? Good grief, she was at least fifty-five! Possibly older. And that was well past the middle of most lives!

"You're not going to need to move in here with me again, are you?" Trying to sound nonchalant, I fought back the panic that I could feel mounting.

"That won't be necessary. If it becomes necessary, I can always stay with Leo."

I wanted to gasp, or was it my gag reflex?

"Let's regroup tomorrow to come up with a plan," she suggested.

"That's a good idea. Beth also wants to help. She is very concerned about being implicated in the murder since she is the one who served Milton and Blanche their salads. You know, I keep thinking back to that day. Everything seemed normal, they seemed normal, she looked well, and so many others had the same salad and were perfectly fine. I bet those needle marks are the key to all this, and I have a hunch that I'm planning to look into tomorrow."

Chapter Ten

I leaped out of bed at the crack of dawn and got right to work. Oh, who are we kidding? It was close to nine before I dragged myself to the edge of the bed and tumbled out, one leg at a time and with a loud moan. I cherished my sleep-ins, which were essential for my thyroid condition. Getting out of bed this early was ungodly but unfortunately necessary.

I tamed my cinnamon colored hair into a tidy ponytail, swiped on some eyeliner and mascara, brushed the fur off my teeth and called Nicole, knowing she'd already be up. Apparently, some people actually enjoy early mornings.

"Do you remember those punk rocker wigs we wore at Halloween?" I got right to the point, lost in thought and really quite unable to use more words than necessary so early in the morning.

"Good morning, Amalia," she said wryly. "I might not remember half the evening, but yes, I do remember the wigs. Why?"

"Can I pop by in the next half hour and borrow

one of them? Actually, I'll take both of them. I need to go under cover."

"I don't like the sound of this, but I know it's necessary for the survival of the bistro, so I won't argue. Truth be told, I'm almost getting used to your snooping. Promise me you won't go alone, though?"

"Beth will be with me for most of the day," I replied, neglecting to mention that she wouldn't actually be with me for the particular outing that I had in mind since she would only arrive after lunch.

"I'm relieved to hear that. I'm here for another hour then I have to head to work at the dance studio." I allowed myself a brief pang of jealousy. Nicole was so graceful and talented whereas I had two left feet (and once upon a time, accidentally packed two left matching shoes when going on vacation, omitting to pack the right shoe!) and no talents that I could think of. I'd long ago been told that drinking wine didn't count, even if I was damn good at it.

I filled Hummer's food bowl, gave him treats and snuggles, assured him he had nothing to worry about and that I'd be home soon. He gave me a shrewd look. He knew me better and clearly did not approve of my plan, however, his concern was brief as he shrugged (I swear!) and turned his attention to his treats.

I was back within forty-five minutes, equipped with a short, black, spikey wig and a platinum, shoulder length, blonde blunt-cut one with black streaks. I dug around in the far corners of my closet until I found my old black denim zipper dress and black hooker boots, the kind that come up over the knee and look bad-ass. I sucked in my gut, wondering in dismay at what point, exactly, I had developed it, and squeezed into the dress. The heavy duty zipper groaned in protest, but I managed to stuff myself into the dress. I attached an ear clip to my right ear and then donned a fake nose ring. Adding more black liner to my eyes and another coat of mascara finished the look. I chose the spikey wig, tucked my hair underneath and surveyed the results.

"Chew talkin' to me?" I said to my reflection in my best Al Pacino tough guy voice then gave myself a Billy Idol sneer. Perfect! I was almost ready. I just had to google some drug terminology so that I could speak the jargon and I'd be all set.

A half hour later, I pulled up in front of the alleged drug dealer's house. Exiting the car, I made my way to the front door, taking time to wipe my nose from time to time and glance about nervously. The nervous bit was genuine, of course, since I was scared sick. I took little comfort in knowing Matt's friend, Ricky, would be arriving soon as backup. He'd stay near the street, but at least I'd have someone close by in case things went horribly wrong. True to his word, Matt had contacted Ricky, who in turn called me just to touch base.

When I mentioned my plans, he begged me to reconsider. When he realized I was determined, he took the address from me, jumped into his car, and assured me he'd be close.

Certain that I was on camera (don't all drug dealers have camera-security and snapping dogs frothing at the mouth?) I took a final cocaine-addict style swipe at my nose and rang the bell. It seemed as though I was waiting forever and I strained to hear the anticipated blood thirsty dogs, but I heard nothing. I almost lost my nerve, but then the image of my floundering bistro emboldened me and I rang again, this time impatiently. The door jerked open and I almost squawked in surprise, convinced that no one would answer.

"Yeah?" A gangly man stared at my snug dress with unconcealed interest.

"I'm here for Mary Jane," I replied boldly. He raised a brow, amused.

"Somehow, I didn't think you were selling Girl Scout cookies," he snickered. "What makes you think I know Mary Jane?" He was toying with me and I knew what he really meant was for me to tell him the name of who was responsible for my presence at his home.

"I'm Blanche's friend," I explained, choosing to use the present tense. "We party together. I'm low on stuff, you know? I've been trying to reach her, but I keep getting her voicemail, so I thought I'd take a chance and come to you directly. She said you're a nice guy…" I swiped my nose again, this time because my allergies were acting up. I fought back a sneeze, afraid that I'd bust out of my dress if I let loose.

"Seems to me you'd be more interested in my

White Pony," he suggested, sizing me up again. I searched my memory bank for the drug terms I'd googled. If I remembered correctly, White Pony was cocaine. He was buying my act. This both terrified and emboldened me.

Evidently, he had decided that I didn't look threatening since he ushered me inside with a sweep of his arm. "You got a name, Blackie?" he purred behind me, thoughtfully providing one for me as I had neglected to think of an alias for myself.

"You seem to know it already," I retorted, "Blanche must have mentioned me then?" I turned and looked at him expectantly as he returned a blank stare. "Blackie, my name," I elaborated.

"Oh, cool. But I don't recall Blanche ever mentioning you. It was just a lucky guess with the black hair and the dress and... So, now that she's dead, you figured you'd deal with me directly, is that the idea?"

I was still being led down a hallway to some type of den. Stopping in my tracks, I whirled around, widening my eyes and letting my mouth hang open. "Dead? What do you mean, dead? We're talking about Blanche from next door, right?" I swiped at my nose again. I could smell man-eating dog and my nose was now twitching non-stop. I was allergic to animals and just barely tolerated my own cat.

"Milton's ol' lady...next door. You did know that she's dead, right?" He squinted at me.

"That's impossible. We're supposed to hang out later. I just ran out of stuff and couldn't wait anymore, like I said. Quit pulling my leg. Oh, I get it, I remember now. Blanche always said you were really funny. You're just playing a trick on me, right?" I tried to sound coy and playful, and then I let my smile waiver ever so slightly. "Right?" I repeated, trying to make my voice tremor.

"You'd better sit down," he said kindly, rubbing a hand nervously along his two-day old stubble. As far as drug dealers went, I found myself quite comfortable with him. Although he was tall, he was not menacing and his features were gentle underneath the stubble. Short, dark hair framed a rather normal looking face with dark, bright eyes. Worry was evident on his face.

"Blanche died a few days ago. I'm sorry; it was in the news and all. You really didn't know?"

I raised a hand to my mouth in mock-shock, blinked rapidly a few times and then dabbed the corner of one eye before shaking my head from side to side.

"I don't really pay attention to the news. That's just awful," I finally squeaked out. Yes, he was buying it, shifting his feet uncomfortably and with a please-don't-cry look on his face. "I can't believe it," I stammered. "Did she over dose?"

"Hell, no! Blanche smoked weed and maybe had a toot every now and then, but nothing that would kill her."

He'd just confirmed that she used cocaine, though probably not often. I felt excitement rippling through me. "Yeah, we tooted together sometimes," I blurted out and then blushed furiously when he raised a brow. I had just made it sound with my awkward wording as if we'd sat around farting rather than doing lines of cocaine. A nervous giggle bubbled up before I could stop it. "I mean, you know, we did blow... I never saw her shoot, but I know she had needles at home." I was fishing for information.

"Blanche was diabetic and had to inject herself with insulin twice a day. She'd been sick lately, too, and had had bloodwork done. Of course, you would know that if you were her friend."

"I haven't known her long," I admitted. "I did know that she had a heart condition, but she never mentioned diabetes to me." I threw in the heart tidbit for credibility. "Do you know how she died?"

"I heard that she ate something nasty at that new bistro on Robin Road, and then she just collapsed face down into her food." I resisted the urge to correct him: she'd eaten, yes, had drunk wine, yes, and then, quite a while later, had keeled over in the parking lot, not face down in her food. "With Blanche gone, it's going to be difficult keeping her old man out of my business. He used to call the cops whenever I had a party, until I became friends with his wife. She managed to convince him to keep his nose to himself."

"You party often, I'm guessing?"

He grinned. "Hell yeah! You should stop by one Saturday night. Wear that dress."

"I've met Milton, too. With Blanche gone now,

I'm sure that he'll be calling the cops on you again," I said, acting as though I was quite familiar with the fat bastard husband. "You don't think the old man offed her, do you?"

"I don't care for Milton, but Blanche was his world. He insisted that she have the best of everything—every comfort. If she was murdered, I'm sure it wasn't by Milton, much as I hate to defend him. I don't see why anyone would kill her though, because she was a nice lady. I've never heard anyone talk badly about her."

"And him?" I urged.

He snorted. "I'd be surprised if there was someone who didn't want to kill him!" He threw back his head and laughed.

"Well, I guess I should be going." I got up from the couch where I'd been sitting and brushed dog fur off my black dress.

"Not so fast!" I looked at him in alarm. Had he finally seen through my act? Had I asked one too many questions? "Didn't you come here for something?"

I shrugged and tried to look sad. "Suddenly, I don't feel like partying anymore, you know?" I replied.

"Well, Blackie, you know where to find me when you change your mind." He followed me to the door and I could feel his eyes taking in every jiggle in my dress. At the door, I merely gave a half-hearted wave and dabbed again at the corner of my eye, as though I were still shedding tears.

Hearing the door close, I practically broke into a

nervous scramble but forced myself to walk slowly, with my shoulders sagging. Once inside the car, I made a show of getting a Kleenex and giving my nose a good blow, in case I was still being watched. As I eased onto the road, a flicker across the street caught my eye. I could almost make out the silhouette of someone standing in the window behind closed blinds.

I sped home as though the devil were on my tail. The mission had been a success. The guy, whose name I hadn't even thought to ask, was definitely not a fan of Milton, but seemed to like, and know, Blanche well enough. Certainly well enough to be convinced that she wouldn't be using needles to shoot up.

Could the needle marks that Nora had heard about simply have been left by her insulin injections or bloodwork? Wasn't insulin normally injected into the butt or the abdomen? Or did someone else inject something into her? More and more, I was convinced that her death had nothing to do with my bistro, and I would not stop until I proved it.

Chapter Eleven

As I parked in my driveway, Ricky pulled up next to me before I even had a chance to open my door.

"Are you crazy?" he whispered angrily, even though there was no one else in the area.

"What?" I asked innocently.

"Do you have any idea who lives in that house?"

"Well, I know he's a drug dealer. He seemed nice enough," I said weakly.

"Amalia, that guy is Eli Hammad." The name meant nothing to me. "Lebanese Mafia," Ricky explained. I paled visibly. "He's been under surveillance for some time. Please tell me you won't go there again. Matt will have a heart attack!"

Distracted, I made a mental note to question the man I saw across the street from Milton's house. I'd take Beth with me next time and wear a different wig. Suddenly, I realized Ricky was looking at me expectantly and that I had tuned out of the conversation. "There's no need to tell Matt about this. Of course I won't go there again, now that I know who lives there."

"I won't say a word because he'd kill me for letting you go anywhere near that place."

I patted his arm. "Honestly, I won't go back there. I got the information I needed."

Ricky sighed as he turned to go. As he walked toward his car, Nora peeled into the parking lot. Bouncing over to where I was standing, she said, "Nice boots. What size are they?" I love that she never questions my attire.

"Size nine, so they'd never fit your tiny feet," I replied, hooking my arm around hers. "Let's eat; I'm famished and I have lots to tell!"

"Do we have a plan of action?" she asked me.

It was nearing noon so I poured her a small glass of Fat Bastard Merlot. Yes, small, since she had to go work for Mr. Leonardo in a couple of hours and I refused to send her there inebriated. She had a loose tongue at times and who knew what she'd say to him if she showed up drunk. She smacked her lips in appreciation. "Is that plums or black cherries I taste?"

"Both," I replied, reading the description from the bottle, "and likely a hint of black pepper. Did you know that this is the wine that inspired me to open the bistro?"

"You never mentioned that. What's the story behind it?" she asked.

"Well, remember my brother Stephen? During the last decade, he's put on a fair amount of weight. As you already know, we have what you could call a love-hate relationship. Well, I saw this particular brand of wine a few years ago and immediately thought of him, because he's fat and he can be not-so-nice at times. I thought it was perfect, but then I began to notice that there were other wines with funny names. After that, it was such a let-down to have a wine with a normal, boring name. And that's how the idea for the bistro was born."

"How is Stephen? He hasn't been here since your parents moved, has he?"

"He's supposed to come for a visit soon. I'm sure he's just enjoying his freedom," I laughed. When my parents lived outside Montreal, he had to visit them once a week. Now that they are here in Robin, it's my turn. So far, it hasn't been too bad. My mom and I had even had some fun when she accidentally signed us up for pole-dancing, thinking it was polish dancing. I smiled fondly at the memory.

I was preparing a cheese platter along with ham sandwiches as I spoke. "Come on, let's get comfortable and I'll tell you what I found out today."

We settled on my favorite couch and ate heartily for a few minutes. I plucked a cube of feta from the pile and popped it into my mouth, enjoying the saltiness for a moment before marrying it with a bite of sandwich. This was my favorite feta, purchased at the Wilton Cheese Factory in Wilton, Ontario. It was so creamy and delectable that I often snuck a few nibbles before bedtime, unable to resist a late night final treat.

Between bites, I briefed Nora on the results of my undercover work. "I'm confused," she said. "It sounds like she was a nice person who got along with everyone. Sure, she liked to get high now and then, but who doesn't?" She took a swig of her wine while I sputtered mid-sip from her comment. "But something doesn't fit. You don't think Milton killed her, do you?"

I shook my head. "No, if he wanted her dead, he would have taken his time when he asked us to help when she collapsed, or he wouldn't have asked for help at all. Plus, he was lucky to have a beautiful, much younger wife who seems to have genuinely loved him. Each time they were at the bistro, they seemed to get along, and there are no rumors about him having financial difficulties, although his clients have lost money. I agree, there is a missing piece to this puzzle." And I think I know what it is, I thought to myself, but chose not to voice my opinion just yet.

"Nora, try to find out more about what killed Blanche, and if there's any question as to Milton's financial status, and finally, see if anyone in particular might have taken a hard financial hit recently."

"Are you thinking that someone might have killed Blanche out of revenge?" Nora asked, her eyes widening.

"It's a consideration," I replied, though it wasn't the one I now entertained. For now, I'd keep my suspicions to myself.

"What about the drug angle? Should I dig into that?"

"No!" I practically shouted. "We don't want the

Lebanese Mafia looking our way. I've heard that they're also responsible for a lot of fires in the Ottawa area. I'd hate for my bistro to be burned to the ground if we rubbed someone the wrong way. And I promised Ricky I'd stay away, and I meant it!"

"What if Blanche rubbed them the wrong way so they rubbed her out?" Nora suggested.

"I sure hope not. The last thing I need is to be on the radar of the Mafia." Sinking ship or going up in flames—I wasn't sure which would be worse. Hopefully I didn't end up on someone's radar after today's visit with Eli. My blood curdled as a sudden thought struck me: what if he'd had someone follow me?

We were both lost in thought when we heard the back door open and then Beth sailed into the room. She smiled at the sight of the food, snagged half a sandwich and sat next to us. "What's the plan for today, boss?" she said.

"If you still want to help, then you and I are going investigating," I replied, wondering if she'd back out

"I definitely want to help. Where are we going?"

"First, I thought we'd go to Milton's house—" I waited politely as a coughing fit overtook Beth. A few minutes later, it finally subsided and she waved me to continue. "Food went down the wrong way. I'm fine. Go on."

"Let's try to meet a couple of Milton's neighbors and see what we can find out. There's one across the street in whom I'm particularly interested. In that house, a man seemed to be lurking behind the blinds and watching the neighborhood. Maybe we can get some information from him. We need a good cover though."

"I know just the thing!" Beth exclaimed. "People keep coming to my door trying to get me to sign up for cheaper electricity. I'm sure it's a scam because the first thing they ask to see is a copy of your recent hydro bill. I'm not sure what they're after because I've always cut them off at that point."

"That would be perfect; you're brilliant Beth! That way, if he doesn't go for it, we can try to strike up a conversation about the neighbors and see if he's at least chatty; or if he does go for it, I'll get his name and maybe I can sweet talk Matt into running a check for me to see if anything suspicious comes up."

"Is there a disguise for me?" Beth asked, eying the get-up I still had on and giving me a nod of approval. "Nice boots," she said.

"I don't think we'll need a disguise this time," I said. "When we go to the old lady's house, I want her to recognize me. Maybe she'll dish out something juicy about Milton. As for the man across the street, I doubt he saw much from that distance while peering between the blinds."

She looked disappointed.

"You can have this if you like," I said, tossing her my spiky wig and giving my head a good scratch. Her face brightened.

"Awesome! I'll go put it on." She disappeared into the bathroom while I went up to my living quarters to change. I didn't want Eli to spot me in the same outfit but with different hair because he'd know that something was up, and I didn't want to end up as food for the ferocious dog that I still imagined he had but had still not seen. I changed into normal clothes, put my hair in a ponytail and went back downstairs to join Beth, now sporting the spikey wig and adorned with pale pink lipstick. She'd put in some cute hair clips and tamed the spikes, and had washed off her eye makeup, too. I rummaged in my office for a moment and came up with a clip board, paper and some pens. "This is the best I can do for a disguise. Let's go."

I parked on the road a few houses past Mrs. Knuedle's house and we walked the short trek to her door, leaving the clipboards behind. They were only needed for the next visit. After ringing the bell and waiting a few minutes, I could hear her screeching from inside. "Just a minute, I'm injured so I can't move fast. Damn Milton!" She yanked the door open as she screamed Milton's name. "Who are you?" she demanded.

"Mrs. Knuedle, I'm Amalia. I called the paramedics for you when you were injured. I just wanted to see how you were doing." I smiled sweetly as she glared at me.

"I suppose Milton sent you to finish me off," she snarled menacingly. I recoiled from the smell of garlic on her breath.

"I hardly even know the vile toad!" I exclaimed. I waited, held my breath. To my surprise, she burst out laughing.

"He does look rather like a frog, doesn't he? Who's this girl?" She nodded at Beth.

"I'm Grace, I work with Amalia," Beth quickly said, surprising me. I didn't think an alias was needed with Mrs. Knuedle. Maybe she was just trying to get into character for the next visit.

"Huh. You could use a little makeup, dear," she said to Beth then waved us inside, limping ahead of us as she led the way.

We were seated on a couch that would probably have been comfortable had it not been covered in plastic. I didn't think anyone did that in this century.

"Mrs. Knuedle, why did you think Milton had something to do with the accident, or that he's trying to kill you?" I asked.

"Cuz he keeps threatening to kill me!" she spat at me, literally. Maybe that's why she kept plastic on her furniture.

"All I do is walk by with my dog and he screams at me from the house about leaving poop in his yard. You want to know the truth? Now, I do leave it, just to piss him off!" She threw her head back and cackled and I couldn't help but grin.

"So there's nothing more to it than that?" I couldn't hide the disappointment from my voice. I was sure she would provide clue. "Did he ever yell at Blanche?" I asked.

"Aha! That's why you're really here." She nodded shrewdly at me. "What's it to you, anyway?"

I sighed deeply and decided to simply lay it out

for her. "His wife dropped dead at the bistro I own, just as they were leaving and walking through the parking lot to their car. They ate the same thing that dozens of others ate that night but no one else died or got sick. Now, everyone's afraid to come to the bistro. I need to figure this out. Nothing makes sense in this case, and the police don't seem to be turning up anything. I'm desperate not to lose my business."

"It was awful," Beth said softly, her eyes tearing.

"Well, I'm sorry to disappoint you, but he doted on her. Why she was with him, I'll never understand since it didn't seem to be for his money. She had money of her own, you know, before hooking up with him." She started to laugh again. "Hooking up with him, get it?" She guffawed and more spittle sailed toward me. I leaned against Beth to avoid it.

I shook my head. "I'm sorry, no, I don't get it." Beth and I looked at each blankly.

"Blanche was a very high priced escort when she first met Milton. Soon after, she quit her job with the escort agency, they got married, and she hadn't worked a day since. She didn't put on airs though and was always kind to others. I liked her."

"How long have you known them?" I asked.

"Only a few months; I moved here last winter."

"What's your take on all this?"

She shrugged. "It's either something from her past, or maybe she wasn't ever the real target."

I was about to speak when Beth pried herself off the plastic, crinkling to her feet. "Thank you very much for your time, Mrs. Knuedle," she said signaling the end of our visit. "Could I possibly use your powder room before we go?"

She went to the small powder room close to the front door as I followed behind Mrs. Knuedle. "Have you seen anything unusual going on around here?" I asked while we waited for Beth to come out.

"Nothing all that unusual: just the voyeur across the street and a drug dealer two doors down. And a few millionaires, too! Or, maybe not anymore, if they invested money with Milton…"

"We were thinking about asking the man across the street a few questions. Is he really a voyeur?"

She shrugged again. "You'll see for yourself."

We thanked her for the information and wished her a speedy recovery then returned to the car for our clipboards. With the amount of trees on Mrs. Knuedle's property, and the angle of the houses, the Voyeur would not have had a good view of us even if he was watching from the window.

"Why did you get up to leave so suddenly?" I asked Beth.

"When it looked like we were out of questions, I figured I'd search her bathroom," she grinned. "So I snooped around, but there wasn't anything interesting, just toilet paper and Kleenex. Actually, it was quite bare."

"It's a big house, Beth. It's just a powder room for guests. I'm sure she has other bathrooms."

"Why would an old lady live in that big house all

alone?" she wondered out loud.

I had to agree with her about that and jotted it down on my clipboard. "Good point, Beth; you're pretty good at this. Maybe we have to do some digging into Mrs. Knuedle, too, as well as look into Blanche's background as an escort. Are you ready?" I nodded to the house across the street and she nodded in return. We walked up the path to the door.

Clipboards clutched to our chests, Beth rang the bell. Almost immediately, the door flung open and a portly man stood there in bright white Fruit of the Loom briefs and a smile on his face. I blurted out the first thing that came to mind.

"Sorry, sir, wrong house…" I grabbed Beth's hand as we hastily walked away. "Hey, come back!" We could hear him calling from a distance. We ran the last few steps to the car and climbed inside as we saw Mrs. Knuedle hobbling down her path with her dog. I could have sworn she was laughing to herself, and I exclaimed out loud, "She knew! She knew that would happen."

"Drive, already, will you?" Beth implored. "What if he comes after us? Drive!"

She didn't have to tell me a third time. The thought of having to see those briefs again made my skin crawl.

Chapter Twelve

"If you ask me, I'd say the escort service is the next place to look into," Beth said as we drove back to the bistro. "I bet there's something in her past that's key to everything."

"But what connection would that have to the bistro? Why did she have to die there as opposed to somewhere else?"

"I'm sure that was just coincidence. After all, the police haven't found any links to the bistro, right?" I nodded sullenly as we pulled into the parking lot.

"I'll just come in and fix my hair. Then I have to go," Beth said, following me into the bistro and heading towards the client washrooms. Although it was Thursday, she wasn't scheduled to work at the bistro, and who knew if I'd have customers anyway? I contemplated putting a sign at the end of the parking lot, advertising a free appetizer with each meal. Would there be any point? Sure, free salad and a side order of death by poison. Come and get it!

I collapsed onto one of the couches and played

back the events of the day in my head, looking for one hidden clue that I was sure had to be there somewhere. I screamed when a furry rat suddenly leaped onto my face then yelled Beth's name furiously as she doubled over laughing.

"You scared the crap out of me!" I fumed, grabbing the wig she'd thrown at me and slapping her with it. "That was so *not* funny!"

"I'm sorry," she gasped for air between fits of laughter. "See you tomorrow," she giggled.

"So not funny!" I yelled at her back.

I grumbled my way back to the kitchen and started pulling out everything I needed to prepare for the evening. Time was running short due to the hours we'd spent investigating.

"Vat the heck!" I said to myself, Hungarian style, and put half the stuff back into the fridge. "I probably won't have more than a handful of people anyway. Oh look, now I'm talking to myself. Great." I took a moment to glare at the ingredients in front of me and wondered if I should even bother cooking a hot dish. My stomach growled the answer to me as a hunger pang slapped me from the inside as if trying to tell me to snap out of my funk. "You're right," I said to my stomach, not even feeling ridiculous for doing so. "I will not sit around and feel sorry for myself." I rolled up my sleeves and set to work.

I was right, though, it was an extremely quiet night.

The next day, I was mincing onions and green and red

peppers as I threw a big mound of lean ground beef and ground pork into a pot. I decided a nice big pot of meaty spaghetti sauce would be just the comfort food I needed, loaded with melted cheese and small, spicy Italian sausage meatballs. Once all the ingredients were simmering, I started on the pepperoni. I'd make pepperoni chips as a little teaser for the customers, free of charge. I sliced the last of it and sighed in frustration. I needed just a bit more but didn't have time to run to the supermarket and the corner store in Robin didn't sell it. Suddenly, I grinned to myself. Yes! I knew where to find pepperoni, didn't I?

Smirking to myself, I quickly grabbed my purse and dashed out the door. A few minutes later, I parked in front of Leonardo's, squared my shoulders and marched inside. Nora stood behind the counter and her jaw dropped at the sight of me. I winked, then held up one hand and counted down with my fingers. Three, Two, One…

Right on cue, Mr. Leonardo stormed out of the kitchen area behind Nora. I glanced at him and with barely a second to spare, narrowly missed being hit by the baton of pepperoni flying toward me. With expert precision, I snatched it out of the air, took a bow, and ran out the door.

After waiting a few minutes to allow my heartbeat to slow down, I poked my head back inside. "Mr. Leo! Do you always have a stick of pepperoni back there just in case I come by?" No sooner had I finished my question than an Italian sausage sailed through the air and slapped me on the cheek. I caught it on the rebound, grinned at Nora and took off at record speed. Victory was mine!

Back at the bistro, I removed the sausage from the casing and formed it into tiny meatballs which I baked before adding them to the spaghetti sauce. I sliced my prize pepperoni and put it into the microwave to turn it into chips. Chloé chose just that moment to arrive: "Who's here?" she called.

"No one yet," I started to reply, then stopped when her purse barked at me. "Chloé?"

"It's my new puppy!" she gushed as a little head popped out of her massive bag.

"Stop! He can't be in here; we're preparing food. Quick, up the stairs!"

Pouting, she headed toward my living quarters with the bag while I followed closely, afraid to see what Hummer's reaction would be and expecting the worst. Safely upstairs, I closed the door to the bistro while Chloé took the small Chihuahua, wearing a little doggie t-shirt, out of her bag and placed him on the floor. "This is Bentley," she cooed with love.

The tiny dog shivered as Hummer ambled into the room. Seeing Bentley, his back arched, and he hissed, and then slowly backed up a few steps to observe the situation from afar. He hissed again but stood his ground. This was his turf.

"I think you'd better put him in the spare room," I suggested. "Is he able to hold his bladder?"

"Uh, kind of?" she asked rather than stated. "I

brought pee pads though, and his crate is in the car. I'll go get it." She shoved Bentley into my arms and we stared at each other while she dashed out to the car.

"You're pretty small, aren't you?" I said to him. He barked in return and gave me a big wet kiss before I could turn my face. "Ack!" I exclaimed, startling him, and then he began to bark excitedly. Hummer kept hissing and I could feel my face start to itch and swell. I was horridly allergic to animals, including Hummer, and in particular to their saliva. Why me? Why today?

"My sauce!" I remembered. I threw Bentley into the spare room and closed the door before Hummer could dash in and eat him then ran down to the bistro. Luckily my sauce was fine, and I gave it a quick stir just as Chloé came in with the crate. I helped her drag it up the stairs and into the spare room, with Hummer hissing at our heels the entire time.

Once Bentley was safely in his crate and pee pads were in place, I breathed a sigh of relief.

"What's that big welt on your face?" Chloé asked.

"That would be from Bentley. He licked me and I'm very allergic to dogs. I'm sorry, Chloé, but why is he here?"

"I just got him today and I couldn't just leave him, he was trembling so much. But I also didn't want to leave you short-handed."

She looked so sad and gave me puppy dog eyes, just like Bentley was doing as he gazed forlornly at us from his crate.

"Thank you for that," I replied, suddenly feeling guilty. "He's very cute. I'm sure my welt will go away once I wash it." I knew it wouldn't and took a quick detour to the kitchen for an allergy pill. This was going to be another long night, I thought to myself.

Sometimes I hate it when I'm right.

Three Meat Spaghetti Sauce

- Small onion, diced small

- Red and green pepper, diced small

- 1 pound of lean or extra lean ground beef

- 1 pound of lean ground pork

- 2 or 3 Italian sausages, removed from the casing (or a package of sausage already out of the casing if your grocery store carries it)

- 2 cans or jars of your favorite store bought tomato sauce

- 2 cans of diced tomatoes

- 1 small can tomato paste

- 1 tablespoon sugar

- 1 teaspoon chili powder

- 2 dashes of cayenne powder. More if you like it spicy

- 1 teaspoon of garlic powder

- ½ teaspoon paprika

- ½ teaspoon dill weed (not seed, the green dried weed)

- ¼ teaspoon oregano

- ½ teaspoon of salt (or more after tasting)

- A sprinkling of ground pepper

In a pot big enough to hold it all, cook the ground beef and pork on medium heat until no longer pink and drain off the fat. Then add the diced onions and peppers and sauté with the meat for a few minutes, until soft. Meanwhile, roll the sausage meat into small meatballs and place on a baking pan. Bake in the oven at 350 degrees for about 20 to 25 minutes or until they look cooked, stirring them around every seven minutes or so.

Back to the pot: once your veggies have sautéd for a few minutes, add the cans of sauce, paste, tomatoes and all the spices. Mix together and reduce to a lower heat and allow to simmer for an hour, stirring frequently so that the bottom doesn't burn. Once meatballs are cooked, remove from the oven and add to the sauce and ensure the sauce continues to simmer for at least thirty minutes after the meatballs are added.

Serve over your favorite pasta and grate your favorite cheese on top. Place each prepared plate into microwave for about 45 seconds for cheeses to melt.

Chapter Thirteen

Perhaps word had gotten around that the night before I'd doled out free booze, or perhaps the people came from out of town; I had no clue, but whatever it was, I was thankful since the bistro was packed. We had a group of young ladies out for a bachelorette party who we sat in the farthest corner of the bistro, but even then we had to remind them to lower their voices when they would start to get out of hand. Helping out, Billy approached their table with eyes as wide as a dear caught in headlights. They had left it up to us to decide on the wine, so I'd told Billy to go with the Live, Laugh, Love and Drink Wine, which he plunked down on their table with a number of glasses, poured quickly, and then hastened back to his safety zone behind the bar.

I frowned. Clearly, he wasn't ready yet to serve the tables. Not a table of pretty, young ladies, in any case. I frowned again as I watched his eyes wistfully follow Chloé around the room. I suspected his heart would soon be broken, either by her or Beth.

I flitted from table to table, handing out small sampler plates of the free appetizers I'd prepared and then rushed back to the kitchen to fill orders. It was a hungry, party crowd and I breathed a sigh of relief. Whatever money I'd lost the day before, I'd surely make up today, and then some.

Nicole rushed into the kitchen, her cheeks glowing. "What a great night for you, Mali! I need four plates of your spaghetti, three of your cheese and salami platter and five of the Feta salad. Do you need a hand back here?"

"Not yet, everything's under control," I replied, sliding three cheese platters toward her and grabbing five salads that were already lined up and ready to go. "I just need to plate the spaghetti, but you can bring these out now." By the time she was back, the last of her orders was ready and I worked quickly to get more salads and cheese platters ready.

After three frantic hours, things finally began to settle down enough for me to venture into the bistro to mingle. There were no familiar faces this evening, proof that this crowd was not from Robin. The bachelorette party was winding down now too, no doubt the girls would be on their way to the nightclubs in downtown Ottawa or the bars across the river in Quebec. With only a few people now remaining in the dining area, I spied a couple of opened bottles of wine at the bar. I took some dessert wine glasses, filled a few to the one ounce mark and gave the remaining patrons a freebie, thanking them for their patronage and introducing myself as the owner.

"It's so lovely here," one older lady gushed. "We're just celebrating our thirtieth anniversary and I've wanted to come here for a while. I read a review about your bistro in the Ottawa Citizen a while back. They were spot on about the ambiance." I glowed under her praise and thanked her, but walking away, a snippet of overheard conversation made me hesitate.

"So this girl shows up, twitchy as heck and wanting some Mary-Jane. She said she was friends with Blanche. Did you know that she died right here at this bistro a few days ago? Oh, geez, I'm sorry. Did you even know that Blanche is dead? I'm such a dolt, you've been away, you probably didn't even know, and I hadn't thought to mention it sooner. I'm so sorry, babe!" He wrapped his hands over hers and launched into his rendition of Blanche falling face down into her salad.

I cringed as I quickly turned my back. It was the Lebanese mafia drug guy, Milton's neighbor, and he was apparently telling his date about my visit to his house. I stole a peek at his date and was stunned by her beauty. She had sleek dark hair and wore trim, stylish clothes. Scurrying away, I knew it was unlikely that I'd be recognized since I wasn't wearing the crazy wig or the clothes, nevertheless I indicated to Nicole to check on their table while I made my way toward Billy at the bar.

"Hey, boss lady, you look beat; why don't you sit down?" Billy suggested, and I suddenly realized how exhausted I actually felt. Out of the corner of my eye, I saw the drug dealer settling his bill with Nicole, and I relaxed, knowing he'd soon be gone.

Just as I was shifting my eyes away, his locked in on me and he gave me an intense look. I smiled politely (after all, I was the owner, and therefore it would be the appropriate thing to do). He was probably silently accusing me of being responsible for his friend's death. The beauty at his side dabbed at her eyes, still reeling from the shock of hearing about the death, I assumed. I reminded myself that there was no way he could possibly recognize me, but the hairs on my neck still stood at attention. I needed a drink. I turned my back and sank onto one of the bar stools. "You're right, Billy; I'm bushed."

"Drink?" he asked, his brow raised.

I forced a grin. "Oh, yes. Surprise me!" I was curious to see what he'd come up with and if he'd caught on to the spirit of matching a mood, situation or impression with an aptly named wine. I burst out laughing at his selection. "Well done, Billy! Put it on my tab," I joked, as I took an appreciative sip of Lucky Night, a rich-tasting Bordeaux with a slightly higher price tag than what I might normally spend.

My lips still at the glass, I sputtered as a hand landed on my shoulder, swept my hair aside seductively, and a gentle kiss grazed my cheek. I caught a fresh and slightly spicy masculine scent that suddenly warmed my blood a degree or two. "Hello," he said, as he eased onto a stool next to me. Relieved that it wasn't the drug dealer, I smiled, turning as red as my wine.

"Nathan! Are you here with your friends again?" I asked this Adonis, noting his casual jeans and crisp white shirt. Suddenly, I felt grubby, smelly and self-conscious. Billy ambled away to the other side of the bar, pretending to be busy.

"Just a couple of them today," he replied, giving me a look that said I was neither grubby nor smelly. This guy would smile his way into my panties if I wasn't careful, I warned myself, succumbing to his grin with a dopey one of my own. "Drew wanted to come by to see if he could convince one of your friends to go out with him." He nodded in the direction of Nicole and his handsome friend on whom she'd had her eye.

"I think he might just get lucky. She did seem taken with him the other night." I guzzled another sip of wine then remembered my manners. "Would you care to join me for a glass of Bordeaux?"

"Whatever you're having…" He watched me lick my lips, his eyes darkening and my blush deepening. I'm having a lucky night, indeed, I thought to myself.

Intuitively, Billy placed a glass in front of Nathan and then left the bottle on the counter between us.

"Do you want me to start tidying up in the kitchen?" he offered, obviously picking up on the vibe or whatever it was between Nathan and me. Unable to speak, I nodded mutely and then Nathan and I were alone. He glanced at the bottle and then chuckled softly. I blushed deep purple in response.

"Are you free to relax with me for a while?" he asked. When I nodded, he picked up the bottle and held out his arm for me. "Follow me," he said gallantly as I tucked my hand underneath his arm, ignoring the screaming little voice in my head that was telling me not to go with him.

He led me to one of the couches, now secluded since there was only one other couple in the bistro other than his friends, who were now chatting with Nicole and Chloé.

"What happened here?" he asked, gently stroking my cheek with a finger. Damn it! I'd forgotten about the welt from Bentley's doggie kiss.

I laughed nervously, confused by the feelings he was arousing in me. "Doggie love. My friend's pooch gave me a kiss and I'm horribly allergic. The welt has gone down quite a bit, though." I fiddled with it self-consciously. Smiling, he leaned toward me, gently kissed the welt, and then settled back onto the couch.

"You're still breath-taking," he assured me, making me suddenly feel as though I truly was, despite my hair being in a pony-tail, smelling of food and wearing my black work clothes. "Tell me about yourself, Amalia. What drove you to open a bistro?"

He said the magic words that suddenly made me feel at ease and I talked passionately about my dreams, the bistro, the hardships I'd faced, even the murders that had taken place. He spoke of his own work and passion for helping people, volunteer work he did in his spare time, his cat and his family.

An hour passed before I noticed Billy dimming the lights, flipping the closed sign over and waving good-bye. I looked about and saw Nicole and Chloé sitting with Nathan's friends. Only the six of us remained. Nicole's eyes caught mine from across the room, and I saw her wink before she returned her attention to their conversation. "It looks like our friends are getting along," I remarked.

"I'm glad. My buddy has been through a rough time lately. It would be good if he met someone nice. His last girlfriend was awful!" He pretended to shudder. "How about you? You haven't mentioned a boyfriend yet." He looked at me questioningly.

A pregnant pause followed. I was suddenly unsure how to answer, mostly confused by my attraction to Nathan and how well we seemed to get along and not wanting to tell him about a boyfriend. "Uhhh," I stammered. "Ahhhh," I guzzled more wine and sighed in frustration.

I had to tell him about Matt.

I raised my eyes, ready to tell all, when his lips gently met mine. My head swirled and I could hear my blood pumping in my ears. Gently, one hand stroked my hair while the other cupped my chin, urging me closer. I couldn't help but respond when the tip of his tongue tentatively sought my own.

"Hey, are you gals having a party?" Nora burst into the room and I leaped away from Nathan, panting. Bless her soul, Nora had the worst timing. But this time, I was reluctantly happy about it.

"I suppose we should join the others," Nathan said, holding my hand and helping me up. I swayed slightly, the blood having left my head and rushed to an entirely different part of my body.

Nora poured herself some wine and strolled toward the foursome as we approached. Phone numbers were being exchanged and Nathan looked at me, questioning. With hands that weren't my own, I found myself scribbling down my number for him. He slipped it into his pocket and then swung his arm around my waist.

"I'm sure these lovely ladies are tired after a hard night's work," Nathan addressed his friends. "Are you all ready to leave?" As everyone said their goodbyes, his lips again met mine softly, briefly. Too brief, however, I should not have allowed it at all. Then the group shuffled toward the door, which swung open just as they neared it.

My heart jumped into my throat.

Chapter Fourteen

"Nathan, I haven't seen you in years!"

Matt and Nathan shook hands then stepped outside to chat. Nicole and I looked at each other in horror. What was he doing back so soon? Why now, when my feelings were all mixed up?! Would Nathan say anything about me? I casually peered outside and saw Nathan and his friends making their way to their cars, and Matt striding across the porch toward the door.

He greeted me with a big hug before I noticed that Ricky was right behind him. Breaking contact, he looked at me sternly. "I heard you had company tonight. Care to tell me about it?"

Oh no! What had Nathan said to him? "I'm not sure what you heard," I started, when he interrupted me.

"Mali, I know that Lebanese drug dealer was here. Don't worry, he's under surveillance. We know his every move. But you should stay out of it. I'd hate for the bistro to go up in flames after all your hard work."

"Wait just one minute!" I sputtered. "First of all, why are you here so suddenly when you're not supposed to be back for days? And for the record, I was in disguise when I visited Eli. In fact, he even casually mentioned it to his date tonight before changing the subject to Blanche's murder, and he made no connection to me or the bistro!"

He sighed in relief. "Are you sure?" I nodded, still waiting for my question to be answered, and then I turned accusing eyes to Ricky, who'd sworn not to tell Matt about my inquiries. He shrugged innocently.

"Why has Ricky been tailing him?" Nicole asked.

"We have an informant in the area," Matt explained. "We've been working with the police to gather information on this guy. We're sure he's involved in a number of things but he always manages to come out clean. We call him Eli the Eel, and Ricky just happened to notice him here tonight and alerted me out of concern for Mali."

I squinted at him. "I thought you were out of town. How did you get here so fast?" He squirmed under my scrutiny.

"I *am* out of town. I wasn't in Ottawa."

"Obviously, you weren't far away?"

"I'm in the middle of a case, Amalia, under cover. I took a big chance coming here."

"Well, everything is fine, Matt. I went to his place in disguise to try to find information about Blanche. As you know, my business is suffering since word got out that she'd been poisoned. That wasn't the case tonight, but tonight was pure luck. Eli himself is spreading stories that Blanche keeled over into her salad, which is entirely false. I didn't know who he was, but trust me, I won't be going there again. His visit here appears to have simply been a date, nothing more, so you can go back under cover." I was suddenly angry, having realized that although he claimed to be out of town, he really hadn't been far away.

"Can we have a word alone?" Matt suggested, gazing toward the kitchen. I stomped ahead of him, leading the way.

Once inside the kitchen, he gave me another hug but my body remained rigid. I was angry at him, confused by my feelings for Nathan, and angry at myself. He sighed deeply. "You know I sometimes have to go under cover and can't tell you about the cases."

"I know, Matt. What I don't understand is why you can't simply be honest with me and at least tell me that although you're under cover, you're close by? Why do you have to make it sound like you're far away when you're really not? And why is it that I don't hear from you for a day or so at a time or that you can't visit if you are close by or at least suggest that I meet you somewhere?"

He ran his hands through his longish hair and gave me a sad smile. My anger wavered slightly, even though I still had the taste of Nathan's lips on my own.

"Sometimes I don't think it's safe for me to say much, and I'm not used to having to answer to someone. I'm sorry. I don't know what else to say."

Fueled by my confusion, the next words out of my mouth surprised even me. "Maybe the timing just isn't right for us to try to be together. I'm not sure I can handle the secrecy, and I don't want to be a burden on you. Maybe I'm just an overly sensitive person. Our relationship has only progressed to a certain point and now it seems to be in a holding pattern." Had Matt and I ever talked as effortlessly as Nathan and I had only moments before?

To my surprise, maybe even to my disappointment, he nodded. "Maybe I'm just too wrapped up in this case and I can't give anything else the time it deserves right now." To his benefit, he did look a bit sad, though not heartbroken. "How about we take a break for now and when this case is over, we can reassess where things stand between us?"

"How long will that be, Matt?" I asked softly.

"I won't lie, Amalia. This is a complicated case. It could be several months."

My heart suddenly felt heavy. He leaned forward and kissed the top of my head, then left while I remained standing in the kitchen. Had we just broken up? Would this have happened if I hadn't been kissed by Nathan earlier? I heaved a sigh as a tear slid down my cheek and stung the welt. If I had been honest with myself sooner, I would have admitted that my relationship with Matt had seemed to stall a month earlier, but that still didn't dull the sadness.

I quickly stole up the stairs to my home to freshen myself. I took out my contact lenses, washed off the last of the makeup that was still clinging to my eyes, stuck my glasses on my face, changed into my jammies and took my thyroid pill. I was just about to join the girls downstairs when I heard a bark. Bentley!

Hummer was on guard just outside the door, trying to peek underneath it. I eased the door open and was greeted by Bentley pouncing at my foot, licking my socked feet. How had the critter escaped from his cage? I looked about the room in a panic, relieved not to see any doggie accidents.

"Good boy, Bentley!" I patted his head, gave him a doggie treat from the pouch Chloé had left on the dresser and peered inside his cage. He'd done his business on the pee pad that Chloé had placed there. I whisked it away, placed it in a plastic bag and put out a fresh pee pad. I threw Bentley's toy into the cage, and after he charged inside after it, closed the door. I know he wanted attention and to play, but frankly, I'd had enough excitement for one day, and he wasn't my responsibility.

"Sorry, you have to stay inside there until Chloé comes to get you." Hummer strolled into the room and gave him a superior look. I swear he was grinning and mocking the poor dog. His tail twitched high and proud.

I trudged back downstairs. Matt, Ricky and Chloé had left while Nicole and Nora waited, chatting quietly. Wait—what? She left?! Apparently, Chloé had forgotten all about her new puppy.

"Sorry girls, my eyes were killing me and I'm exhausted and… Matt and I just broke up." They murmured gentle words of sympathy but I could see

Nicole's eyes sparkling. She had seen Nathan kiss me but wouldn't bring it up in front of Nora.

"Are you going to be okay, Mali?" Nora asked with concern. "You did look quite cozy with that delicious guy, Nathan. Did that have anything to do with the breakup?" Apparently, not much manages to escape Nora's beady eyes and sharp mind.

"I'm fine, really I am. To be honest, it had kind of fizzled out between Matt and me lately. I just didn't want to admit it to myself. We agreed to meet in a few months to talk. No promises. Maybe the timing just wasn't right."

"Are you ready for some news, then?" she asked, rubbing her hands together in excitement.

Chapter Fifteen

I could tell that Nora was bursting at the seams with whatever news she had to share. She squirmed with excitement, my break-up already forgotten.

"This isn't going to be anything gross about Mr. Leonardo's back hair again, is it?" I asked cautiously, mentally preparing to gag.

"Oh that man!" she exclaimed, her brown eyes turning into daggers. "Did you know he's been telling everyone not to eat here because they'll be poisoned? The nerve! If he wasn't so damn handsome, I would have walked out on him tonight. But don't worry, Mali; whenever I can, I set people straight. That man is such a gossip. It's a good thing that I'm working there for a few days so I can diffuse the situation." Her face beamed with a sense of purpose and self-satisfaction.

I should have been angry but at this point I was beyond exhaustion. "How, exactly, is he suggesting that I'm poisoning everyone, and what in the world would my motive be?"

"That's a good question, Mali, I'll have to stick that one to him tomorrow." She whipped out a notepad and scribbled furiously. "What could you possibly gain by poisoning people? He has this hair-brained idea that you're growing poisonous plants in your garden. How would he even know that you have a garden?"

I knew how he knew. A few months back, I had stumbled across information suggesting that he and the former owner's wife had been having an affair, so he was no stranger to my property. Did he know something I didn't know?

"Most of the plants were already here when I bought the place. Harriet, the former owner, had little stakes in the ground with the botanical names on them. I bought a few things and added to the garden, but nothing dangerous… I'm really no expert. Other than that, I brought my potted Oleanders with me when I moved here, which I've had for years. I don't think they're poisonous, are they?" Both looked at me blankly and shrugged. "I'll look into it tomorrow and research every plant I have. Does this mean that the police seem to have narrowed it down to some type of plant poisoning?"

"That is exactly what's being said in the rumor mill, and the reason why Leo is focusing on that to muddy your name. Take a good look at that garden tomorrow, Mali, and if there's anything there that might be poison, let the cops know right away. I'll keep my ears to the ground."

"I wonder why the cops haven't come to look at

my garden yet," I mused out loud, "unless, of course, the exact toxins haven't been identified yet. Yes, I'll do that first thing in the morning, and after that, I have to look into the high-end call girl business."

Nicole's eyes, which had begun to drift shut, popped wide open. "Are you low on cash because business is down lately? Surely, you had a great night tonight." Her brows knit together with sudden worry as she waited for my answer. I burst out laughing.

"I'm not job hunting, silly! Word has it that Blanche was a call girl before hooking up with Milton, no pun intended. I thought I'd poke into that a bit to see if she had enemies or stalkers. So far, she's come up smelling like a rose. If this doesn't pan out, I'll have to sniff down some other leads, but I want to put this one to rest first. And speaking of rest, my apologies, but I've got to go to bed. It's later than usual; you're both welcome to sleep here, if you like," I offered, noting Nicole's eyes fluttering shut again.

"I'll take you up on that," she said gratefully, heaving herself off the couch. Nora had the good grace to blush as she murmured her decline. I knew where she'd be heading next, and visions of hairy backs danced grotesquely in my head, prompting me to ponder if her back might be hairy too.

Nicole and I dragged ourselves up to my place and grunted a good night at each other as we made our way down the hall. A bark stopped me in my tracks. Bentley! Before I could open my mouth, Nicole opened the door to the spare room and Bentley dashed through her legs, with Hummer in hot pursuit. Not even noticing, she staggered to the bed and crawled under the covers, fully clothed, while I chased the animals. Seeing Hummer's favorite stuffed dog, Bentley abruptly scooped it up in his mouth, ran into my room, and headed straight under my king-size bed.

Hummer stalked him from the sidelines, peering underneath the frame and hissing. I ran back to the spare room, grabbed the dog treats and promptly stepped into a pile of something cold and squishy that oozed between my toes. *Bazd meg*!

Hopping on my one clean foot, I made my way to the bathroom and stuck my foot directly into the bathtub, poured half a bottle of shampoo over it and blasted it with the hottest water I could handle. Once clean, I slathered antibacterial lotion from my toes to my knees, then repeated, all the while exclaiming, "Ew, ew, ew!"

What a crappy day this had turned out to be!

I stomped to the kitchen, grabbed a bag of cat treats, and then shook the bag and waited. Within seconds, both critters came running, and to my complete amazement, sat down side by each, looking at me expectantly, their tails wagging. I placed a treat in front of each and each gobbled it and waited for more. I switched things up this time and put a cat treat down for Bentley and a dog treat for Hummer. Bad idea, I soon found out, as Hummer arched his back and hissed. Bentley ate it anyway, and then I snatched him up and wrestled him back into his impeccably clean crate.

Despite his whimpering, Nicole slumbered on. I turned on the light to clean the squishy mess, which took the better part of ten minutes for a thorough cleaning. Again, I muttered, "Ew, ew, ew!" through the entire process. How could Chloé forget her dog? And how in the world could Nicole continue to sleep through all this?

I finally fell into my own bed at 3:00 a.m., exhausted to the core. In what seemed like only a few minutes, a woodpecker began his peck-peck-pecking noises, and I groaned as I opened an eye, only to discover daylight streaming in through my blinds which I hadn't closed. Barking and hissing joined the pecking sound, and I pulled a pillow over my face, trying to recapture the erotic dream that I had been in the middle of when I realized the pecking was actually a soft knocking on the door.

I stumbled to answer and, despite the early hour, was happy to see Chloé at the door. Thank God, I'd soon be rid of the pooping pooch!

"Sorry to wake you Amalia," she said, looking frantic. "Did I leave my wallet here? I can't find it any-where!" Incredulous, I searched for words that wouldn't offend her but had difficulty biting my tongue.

"Maybe it's in the spare room…with your *dog*? Haven't you noticed that he was missing?" Admittedly, I took morbid pleasure at watching the color drain from her face as the realization set in. Sadly, the moment was short lived as Nora came bustling inside too, humming softly to herself. She strolled right into the kitchen and started to make coffee.

Just then, Nicole came staggering out of the guest room, hopping on one foot, saying "Ew, ew, ew! What's on my foot?"

Then, as if in slow motion, Bentley the little Houdini dashed around her and practically climbed up Chloé's pant leg. She glared at me. "Did you let Bentley roam around your place all night? He's not fully trained, you know!"

"Trust me, I know," I replied, exchanging a sympathetic look with Nicole. "Your precious Bentley, however, knows how to get out of his crate and is fond of leaving little presents." With that, I handed her the bucket and cleaning supplies and pointed at the guest room, none too politely. Her jaw dropped in surprise.

"I haven't had coffee, I only slept a few hours, Matt and I broke up yesterday, I've stepped in your dog's crap and cleaned it up once already, and I have a gagging problem, I might add, so it was no treat. I'm not cleaning up another mess that came out of this dog, which you seem to have forgotten exists." With that, I stomped back to my room, slammed my door, closed my blinds and went back to sleep.

I am not a morning person.

I awoke at the much kinder hour of 11:00 a.m., feeling suitably refreshed. Cautiously sticking my head out of the bedroom, I listened. Silence! Just to be sure, I tiptoed to the kitchen like a ninja and then froze, listening again. Blessed silence! I brewed coffee, noting three mugs already washed on the drying rack. I poured sugar and cream into one of the mugs and willed the pot to work faster. Finally, it was ready and I took my first fortifying sip. Ah, sanity!

Now mentally alert, I tucked right into my research, firing up the lap top. To my horror, I discovered that I had three, and possibly six, poisonous plants in my garden.

Chapter Sixteen

My beloved Oleander! Who knew? I felt as though I had just been betrayed by a dear, old friend. And the innocent white Lily of the Valley that I used to pick as a child and put in glasses of water for my mother! My bright pink Foxglove, with their plethora of cheerful little heads. Some forms of Milkweed were toxic and they grew rampant along the hiking trails next to my property. I gasped when I read that even the Coneflower and their relative, the Black Eyed Susan were toxic (I had recently planted some, though they weren't yet in bloom). My garden was a smorgasbord of toxins, ready for picking.

The question now was how had any of these ended up in only one salad, and why Blanche's salad? I had assembled and plated the salads myself. Was Blanche even poisoned at Whine and Cheese? And how would the poison have such an effect so quickly? And was it even intended for her? Maybe something in her past held the key to such questions, I reasoned, so I quickly made a list of escort services (who knew there were so many?) and the addresses. It was time to do some real digging.

My first task of the day would be a chat with Officer Lynette. Where had I put her card? That's right, I'd never had it, Nicole did. I chuckled to myself as I remembered Lynette hitting on Nicole. I called Nicole to get the number, squared my shoulders, and then called Lynette. To my surprise, she answered on the first ring.

"Officer Lynette, this is Amalia, from the Whine and Cheese. I was wondering if you could stop by. I believe I have something that might interest you." She agreed to be at the bistro shortly.

I rushed down to the restaurant, unlocked the front door and tidied up while I waited. Hesitating in front of my display cabinet, I noted that it needed updating. I would have to make it more summery and I had a sudden inspiration as I remembered my new cheese boards. They would look fabulous on display and after receiving many compliments on them, I was sure I could sell a few as well.

Placing a few boards inside the cabinet, I then added some packages of tropical colored napkins, new wine glass charms that my good friend Sue had just finished making for me, and some summer-themed wines like Barefoot, Rose Flamingo (which just looked so summery), Fun and Playful, and Levity. I had also just received a shipment of quirky wine glasses that I hadn't yet opened, so I went to my storage room/office and retrieved a box, removed four glasses and added them to the cabinet. On each glass were three lines. The two-ounce mark indicated "usual day"; the four-ounce mark, "tough day"; and the six-ounce mark, "I don't want to talk about it".

Did I mention that these were very big glasses?

I was positioning the last glass when the officer tapped on the door.

"Thank you for coming so quickly. Let's go back to my garden, if you don't mind?" I silently led the way.

"This is cozy," she commented, plunking herself down onto one of the chairs. "What a great spot to have a drink. If only I wasn't on duty." She sighed wistfully. "So, what is it that you wanted to show me?"

I took a deep breath for courage. "I've heard through the grapevine, otherwise known as the evil Mr. Leonardo from the pizza place down the street, that Blanche was reportedly killed by an unusual poison. He's been telling everyone who will listen that it likely came from my garden. Actually, he's been telling people that I'm poisoning my customers. That got me thinking, of course. For one, he's been here, so he would know about my garden. You see, he was....friends....with the former owners. I've never had a garden before, so I became curious and did some research." I took another deep breath. "It seems we're sitting in a sea of poisonous possibilities." I bowed my head sadly.

To my surprise, she barked out a laugh. "Is that all? We already know all that! I'm curious, though, about how Mr. Leonardo knows it too."

"It seems that the police who go into the pizzeria talk freely amongst themselves about their cases, and he's apparently happy to pass along his own version of what he's heard. Especially if it involves slandering me," I replied testily.

"You're right; many of the plants here are toxic. If you search deeper though, you'll find that many common plants and herbs are toxic. In this case, since the word seems to be out, and since it will be in the news soon, yes, Blanche seems to have ingested a number of the toxins found in plants here in your garden. During the times we've been here looking around, we did take samples of all of them. Keep in mind, though, that many people have these same plants in their gardens, and that we've already established that you have no connection to Blanche or to Milton and would not gain from her death, although we're still investigating your staff and everyone who was here that day."

I was surprised by the amount of information that she freely shared, including that I had been under investigation myself and unaware of it. "May I ask how you determined my innocence?"

"We work closely with Matt and his friend Ricky on another matter. They've both vouched for you, and of course the department is already familiar with your involvement in previous cases. No offense, but you seem to have a way of attracting death to your doorstep. The cops all think that it's bad luck to come here!" She laughed smugly; I was not amused.

"That's ridiculous!" I sputtered. For some reason, I was also a little irked that I'd been so easily dismissed as a suspect based merely on Matt's word. "Just for the record," I added, "Matt and I broke up last night."

She nodded. "Probably for the best…" With that, she took her leave as I continued to brood. How did she know what was best for me? A pang of hunger roused me and I heaved myself into the bistro for a bite to eat.

I made myself a mix of feta cheese, firm, diced tomatoes and radishes, sliced green onions, chives from my garden that I hoped weren't toxic, chopped dill weed, cilantro and chopped, spicy Mexican salami, drizzled and tossed with olive oil and laid onto slices of crusty baguette. My spirits quickly lifted as the salty taste tantalized my tongue. Life was good again.

While brushing my teeth, I contemplated my wardrobe. What would a high-priced escort wear during the day? Something classy but casual? Or would the daytime look be more ghetto-raunchy? I glanced inside my closet. I had no clothes to fit the occasion. Expensive was not in my budget, nor was raunchy within my comfort zone.

My eyes landed on a full-length summer dress that was mainly black but with splashes of pastel green and yellow. I had recently worn it to a wedding and had had many compliments, even though the dress had cost less than fifty dollars. It would have to do. I slung some strappy black heels onto my feet to complete the look and rushed out the door before I lost my nerve.

By now I knew that I was terrible at finding my way around downtown Ottawa, so I punched the first address into my trusty GPS and set off eastbound. I got off the freeway at the Nicholas exit, went straight, made a few right and left turns, and then parked the car in a nearby parking lot.

I had walked into three questionable places already, certain that they weren't where Blanche would have worked, made some half-hearted inquiries and left dejected before deciding to try one last place. Locating the building, I took the elevators to the tenth floor then walked into what looked like a regular business office with a cozy reception area and waiting room chairs scattered about a focal point coffee table littered with magazines. The only indication that this was not a typical business office was that the magazines were racy. I felt my first tremor of nervousness.

I approached the desk, and when the receptionist looked up, my breath hitched in my throat. I could be mistaken, but she looked like the beauty that Eli the drug dealer had been with the previous night at the bistro! I exhaled sharply. Thank goodness I'd decided to wear a long, red-haired wig that I'd found in my closet. I cleared my throat nervously. "Hello. I was wondering if, by any chance, you are hiring?" I willed myself to look straight into her eyes.

She gave me a long look, right down to my strappy shoes. I must have passed inspection and I thanked my lucky stars that, despite my thyroid condition, I had only gained a few pounds and was still relatively fit. Just for good measure, I subtly sucked in my stomach a tad. "What type of position are you interested in?"

"I assumed there was only one kind, but perhaps I'm mistaken. A friend of mine, who recently passed away, had mentioned this place and that she used to earn a good salary. I could use some extra cash."

"Oh? Who was your friend?" I had her full attention now.

"Blanche," I began, then faltered. I could not remember her last name, if ever I knew it.

"Isn't it tragic," she responded. "She was such a class act. Even after she left us, she kept in touch." She smiled briefly. "In fact, I met my current boyfriend through her. To begin the process, you can complete these forms and then I'll schedule a meeting with Madame LaJambe." She shoved a pile of forms my way.

"Thank you so much," I forced myself to gush. "I'm Syrah." I cleverly used the name of a varietal grape that came to mind and stuck my hand out for her to shake, subtly forcing her to divulge her own name. I was becoming good at this.

"Ebony," she replied, tossing her sleek mane.

I sat amongst the girly magazines and completed the forms with fake information. "So you must have known Blanche well, if you met your boyfriend through her," I prodded casually.

"Quite well, actually. After she married Milton, she would have some of us over to her place for parties. Sometimes it was just a few friends getting together, but sometimes it was a working party, if you know what I mean. Her husband knew a lot of wealthy people from out of town. Well, just a few weeks ago, she invited me to a party at her neighbor's house, and it turned out to be Eli, who I'm now dating. I found out only yesterday that she was poisoned at the bistro where we were eating!"

I cringed at her wording but resisted the urge to correct her. "You know, I've met Milton a number of times, but she never mentioned how they met. Did they meet here?"

She scrunched up her face, thinking. "You know, I can't recall if she met him through us, or if it was through her friend Lea Gregson, who also worked here." She shrugged then dismissed me to answer the phone.

Lea Gregson? Could that be Greg Gregson's current wife? I stored that little tidbit away for now as I handed Ebony my forms. As she hung up the phone, I politely asked if I should wait around for a meeting with Madame LaJambe, or if I should expect to be called at a later date.

"She's quite busy today, however I would not be surprised if she came out of her office for a quick look at you. I'll see if she's available now."

She was back in just a few minutes with the tallest lady I'd ever seen. She was all legs and I was convinced that LaJambe could not possibly be her real name but a very suitable assumed name. She shook my hand warmly, then circled about me, much like a hungry shark, then nodded.

"Syrah… What a splendid name you have. I'm afraid I can't discuss future employment with you now, but I'll have Ebony call you for an appointment, perhaps early next week."

"Thank you," I murmured, knowing I'd never get the call since I had given an incorrect number. No matter, I had already gleaned that Blanche was well liked and respected here, and that Mrs. Gregson might be a person of interest. I still had some questions, though. "My condolences regarding Blanche," I offered. "It must have been a shock to everyone here."

"Ebony told me about her death just this morning. We'd both been out of town at a convention in Las Vegas. It was quite a shock." Her eyes misted over.

"I can't understand why anyone would want to kill her. She seemed to be on good terms with everyone." I lied freely without batting an eyelash.

"The clients were all fond of her, too. She made everyone feel special. It was a shock when she married that older man and stopped working. She'd still come in at times though, filling in for Ebony at reception. She liked keeping in touch with everyone, even the clients."

"No one that I can think of had ill-will toward her," I commented one last time without sounding as if I were prodding. My effort paid off.

"Except for Lea's husband," Ebony blurted, and then clamped a hand over her mouth as Madame glared at her. "Sorry, I shouldn't have said that. So, I will be in touch in the coming days, Syrah." She smiled tightly and returned to the sanctity of her desk, while Madame and her legs click-clacked away in incredibly high heels. I left the office, took the elevator to the lobby, waited a few minutes, and then went back up. I slithered into the office and whispered to Ebony, "Sorry, I didn't mean to get you in trouble. I just want to check which phone number I gave you. I recently moved and I suddenly couldn't remember if I wrote the right number?" She rattled off the number I'd provided and, with a courage I didn't quite have, I corrected her with my proper number. I had a feeling I'd still have more questions once I considered everything I'd gleaned so far, and that I'd want to return. My cell number was unlisted anyway, so they wouldn't be able to use that to find information about me. I'd make sure to change my voicemail greeting as soon as I left the building, to ensure also that my name wasn't mentioned. I turned to leave and in my haste almost bumped into a man entering the office. I excused myself and continued on my way. Once the elevator doors closed, I exhaled deeply.

Eli had stared directly into my eyes.

Chapter Seventeen

I made it back to the bistro just in time to prepare the platters before we opened. I was still haunted by Eli's deep and searching gaze into my eyes. Was he following me, or was he merely visiting his girlfriend? Could he have recognized me? I would have to be more careful.

Absorbed in my thoughts, I jumped when a knock sounded at my back door. Solid steel, a gift from my parents following some break-ins, there were no windows to peer out. "Who is it?" I yelled through the door.

"Nathan," came the muffled response. My loins twitched.

I opened the door and peered out, a silly grin on my face that I could not contain. His face wore the same type of silly grin. He stood there, in his paramedic outfit, holding a bouquet of multi-colored roses. I searched my memory. Had Matt ever brought me flowers? I couldn't recall, but I knew that I shouldn't compare.

Judy Volhart

Nathan held the flowers out to me. "Sorry, I didn't know where to knock. I knocked on the front door but I don't think you heard, so then I tried upstairs and finally back here. I didn't want to leave the flowers out here in the heat. These are for you."

"Thank you, they're beautiful! This might be only the second time in my life that I've received flowers. Do you have time to come inside?" I could feel myself blushing.

"I'm due at work soon, but I couldn't wait to see you again." He grinned again, suddenly shy now that he'd shown his feelings. Without hesitation, I stepped toward him and gave him a kiss that left both of us panting. "Wow!" He gave me a tender, bewildered, and searching gaze, then leaned in for more. Our tongues circled gently, shyly becoming acquainted then more aggressively, possessively exploring. We both jumped when the back door burst open. Nora, bless her soul, who had her own key...

"Well, helllo," she purred, batting her eyes at Nathan and then raising a brow in my direction. Nathan politely responded then whispered to me, "When can I see you next?"

"After tonight, I'm free for the next two days."

"Tomorrow for dinner then?" he suggested. After my nod, he gave me a gentlemanly peck on the cheek and took his leave. I turned to face Nora.

"Your timing sucks, you know..."

She shrugged. "I wish I could say that it's the first time I've been told that. But you're going to love me

132

when I tell you what happened today!"

"Have you already worked a shift at the pizza place?"

"Yes, and I'm done for the day so I thought I'd pop over for a drink," she hinted none too subtly. I waved her into the bistro.

"After you; my bubbling fountain of information." I followed behind and giggled to myself as she practically vibrated with excitement, her silver ponytail trembling.

Her hands shook as she accepted a glass of wine. "That lady police officer you mentioned came by and spoke with Leo in the kitchen, but I could hear everything! She grilled him about how he knows about what poisons may have killed Blanche and why he seems to be so familiar with what's in your garden. She was relentless, and he got so flustered that he almost forgot how to speak English!" She giggled then took another swig from the glass.

"He admitted to being friends with the former owners and thus having been in your garden, but adamantly claimed not to have set foot in your place since it had been sold to you. Then she blasted him for spreading rumors about you and casually dropped such words as 'slander' and 'defamation of character' and then not so casually told him point-blank that she didn't want another word out of his mouth regarding you, the bistro or poisons. By then, he was so shook up that he just stood there nodding and repeating 'Yes, ma'am, yes!' He hasn't left the kitchen since."

I grinned at the image of Mr. Leonardo, shaken

and flustered. He deserved it about as much as he deserved being smacked upside the head with a bat of his own pepperoni. I vowed, one day, to do that.

I shared my findings about the call girl agency and the revelation about a possible link with Mr. Gregson and his presence at the bistro the day of the murder. "Ebony seemed to think that he might have reason to dislike Blanche. I was thinking jilted lover, perhaps…"

Nora's eyes shone with excitement. "I'll bet that's what it is. Maybe he was a former client of hers, fell in love, but then Milton stole her away, and because of Milton he also took a hit to his investments. Double whammy!"

It was an interesting theory, but it didn't feel right. "Let's put this on the backburner for now and get to work," I suggested, heading to the bistro doors to open them while she downed the last of her wine.

I'd no sooner unlocked the doors when Milton burst into the bistro and made a beeline for the restroom. When he emerged, he was sweating profusely. He fixed his beady eyes on me then marched over to me and plunked down ten one hundred dollar bills. "This is yours if you let me go back into your kitchen and fix my own plate of food. I'm starving, and I think someone's trying to poison me, too. I'm afraid to use my own kitchen or to ask my cook to prepare something."

I blinked in surprise then smiled sweetly. "Right this way, Milton. Be my guest." Hey, everyone has their price and a thousand dollars is a lot of money for someone like me. I brushed my pesky conscience aside, scooped up the cash then led the way to the kitchen. I handed him a plate and gestured to the prepared dishes of salamis and cheeses. He fell upon the food as though he hadn't eaten in weeks, heaping his plate full, then took a seat in my office. Feeling a pang of sympathy, I brought him a bottle of wine and a corkscrew.

"You can open it yourself so you'll know it hasn't been tampered with." I held out a bottle of Fat Bastard to him. He accepted it but waved away the glass that I also offered. Almost as quickly, he changed his mind and beckoned for me to approach. He filled the glass halfway, then nodded at it. "Drink up," he commanded, squinting at me suspiciously. Who am I to argue? I took a long sip and only then did he take a grateful swig directly from the bottle.

I let him eat in silence for a few minutes before daring to speak. "Why do you think someone's trying to poison you?"

He continued to chew ravenously, ignoring me for a few moments. I forgave him: I likely would have behaved the same, had I been starving. "The salad that Blanche ate," he started, then paused as a flicker of sadness crossed his face, "was mine." I remained quiet, sensing that he had to enlighten me at his own pace. Several minutes passed before he continued. "I was just about to take a bite when she insisted we switch, because mine had more strawberries. So that

135

salad was intended for me. Do I know who's after me? It could be anyone. I know many people, and many of them wouldn't be sad to see me dead. Who would have access to the food at your bistro is what's most perplexing."

"Listen, why don't we team up?" I suggested tentatively. "You can come here every day for supper, to fix your own plate of food, and we can exchange ideas and information. Maybe together we can figure this out." He turned a questioning eye in my direction. "I've solved a couple of mysteries in the past," I explained.

"It seems I don't have a choice, Missy," he conceded after consideration.

I jumped at the opening. "Tell me about Greg Gregson." I didn't bother to correct him about my name. For some strange reason, I'd gotten used to being called Missy.

His face contorted with disgust. "Greg? Why is his name the first one that pops out of your mouth?" Suddenly, his face cleared, as though a fog had lifted. "He was there that night." He now looked at me with a new admiration. "Perhaps there's more to you than meets the eye. Greg and I go way back. We'd travelled in the same circles, dated the same women," he flashed a grin that faded just as quickly. "He was seeing Blanche quite regularly when I came along. He was paying for the pleasure of her company, of course. After one paid evening with me, we agreed to start dating and she stopped working as an escort."

He watched my face closely for a reaction. "I assume you already know some of this, if you're as intelligent as I'm beginning to think you are?"

I gently prodded him to continue. "Were there ill feelings after that?"

"He was in a rage at the time, but that was a while ago now. He started dating his current wife soon after, but we were never friendly again. Unfortunately, the market took a downward turn at about the same time. He still had investments through my firm and he lost quite a bit of money. Naturally, he blamed me, even though I, too, lost millions."

"Might that be a reason to want to harm Blanche? Or kill you?" There, I'd said it. He stared at me for several moments before opening his lips to speak.

"You are on the same wavelength as I am. I'm positive that I was the intended victim, as I told you earlier. Greg would still try to contact Blanche, wanting to win her back, despite his marriage. If I were dead, then he could have been there to comfort Blanche, possibly get her to fall in love with him. He would not have wanted her dead, of that I'm certain. That plate was meant for me. The only question is: if not Greg, then who is the killer?"

I felt increasingly confident that our theory was correct and that Blanche's poisoned plate was indeed meant for Milton. That's why nothing had made sense up to this point, and why the puzzle pieces had not fit together.

"Why do you think someone is still trying to kill

you? And why don't you trust your staff? Do they have ill feelings toward you?"

He blushed and lifted a corner of his rubbery lips in a smile. "Really?" I couldn't help but to exclaim out loud.

He grinned at me slyly. "This old fox still has some moves. I haven't slept with all of them," he hurried to add.

"Is that because some of them are male?" I couldn't help but retort, unable to keep the disdain from my voice. To my surprise, he burst out laughing.

"Touché, Missy! You are both clever and witty. Now, what's next?"

"Your staff. Could I have a list of their names and addresses, as well as anyone that may have quit in the past year with whom you slept? And while we're at it, could I have Mr. Gregson's address as well? Actually, let's also add anyone else to that list that you think should be a prime suspect. Didn't the police ask you for something like this?"

"Of course they did. But they still seem convinced that Blanche was the intended victim, so they're just wasting time. They refuse to accept that I was the intended victim. I understand that they have already spoken with Greg. It seems that he was quite emotional when talking about Blanche, but he apparently did not implicate himself."

"What about his wife? Does she have ill feelings toward you?"

"Not that I know. She's actually a very nice lady. I

also don't think that she knows he was still hung up on Blanche, but I'm just guessing. Why would she stay with him if she knew?"

"Did Blanche know about you and your staff?" I blurted out, unable to stop my nosiness.

"If she did, I don't think she cared. She's never mentioned anything to me and she was always kind to the staff."

"Why did you cheat on her?" I couldn't help myself but I knew I was pushing limits.

He seemed to have a hard time finding the words. "I guess I figured, being as beautiful as she was, she was probably cheating on me too, so why not? If they were willing, I was able. I'm still very virile, you know." He gave me a smarmy grin and I recoiled.

"Did you ever know for certain that she cheated?"

"No. I was just speculating." He blew out a long sigh. "In all honesty, she probably never did cheat on me. I was an idiot." With that, he rose, grabbed the pad of paper I'd given him and nodded curtly at me. "Thank you for your hospitality. I'll get those names and addresses for you. You may stop by tomorrow afternoon to get the list."

With that, he was gone.

Chapter Eighteen

I could barely sleep that night and finally gave up by seven in the morning. I was anxious to get the list from Milton, and even more anxious to get ready for my date with Nathan. My feelings were reminiscent of the anticipation and excitement that one feels at Christmas time. The image of our last kiss kept replaying in my mind, bringing a blush to my cheeks and a grin to my face. I had gotten more than one odd stare the night before from walking around smiling to myself, but I simply could not contain it.

I was carefully planning my wardrobe for the evening when the doorbell rang. I scowled, wondering who would visit me this early; anyone who knew me well knew that I'd usually still be sleeping. I peered out the door and froze, my previous grin replaced by a frown. I opened the door tentatively. "Matt? What are you doing here? And why so early?"

He took a step toward me, arms held open. Stunned, I took several steps backward. He looked wounded as he lowered his arms. "I've missed you,

Amalia. Breaking up was the wrong decision. I know that now. Not seeing you is driving me crazy."

"Matt, I don't know what to say. I'm sorry, but I disagree. I think that we made the correct decision and, well…I've met someone else." I hadn't meant to blurt it out like that. He flinched, as if I'd slapped him.

"What? That's impossible. It's only been a couple of days since we broke up!" The wounded look returned, along with one of irritation.

"Matt, the truth is that we weren't right for each other. Our differences were really coming to light, especially during the past few weeks. I know that I couldn't stand you being away or under cover and not being able to tell me where you were or anything about the case. That's not how I want to live my life. I need someone who will be there for me when I need him. Separating is for the best."

"I didn't expect this. I feel so foolish now."

Before I could respond, he turned abruptly, bounded down the stairs and moved swiftly across the parking lot to his car. I watched sadly, knowing that while I was very fond of him, I hadn't truly been in love with him. I watched from the window until his car left the lot, silently wished him well, and then closed the door on that chapter of my life.

I slunk back to my room feeling lower than a snake belly and half-heartedly finished choosing my outfit for my date with Nathan. He made me feel light, sexy, and happy, and I tried to choose an outfit that reflected those feelings. I chose a yellow sundress that flowed to my ankles and accented all my best features while covering up my bumps and blemishes. I wondered just when I'd gained the few pounds that now seemed to pad my waist and butt. Damn thyroid!

I forced myself to relax with a cup of coffee while killing time. In reality, I wanted to rush over to Milton's place for the list, but it was still too early. I paced a while before turning on my computer for a look at recipes and ideas for the bistro that were posted on Pinterest. Around eleven o'clock, I sped off to Milton's house. To my surprise, he opened the door himself, smiled, reached into his pants pocket, waggled his caterpillar eyebrows, and then pulled out a piece of paper. He half-bowed as he handed it to me.

"Missy, not sure what took you so long, but we've got work to do. Between you and me, this isn't the same list I gave to the cops. Since then more names have popped into my mind. I also categorized them for you. See, here, all these names are staff or former staff, these are clients…" He droned on, but I had tuned out; I was staring in disbelief at the long list of names of staff and ex-staff members. Surely this wasn't all the women he'd slept with. But I was not here to judge, and I'd do well to remember that. "I even put it in order of most probable," he continued, oblivious that I hadn't been listening.

"Thank you, Milton. That was very pro-active," I replied courteously. "Now tell me, if you had to narrow it down to only one category of acquaintances, which would it be?"

He stuck out his tongue between his wormy lips as he contemplated my question. His beady eyes squinted in concentration and then his nostrils flared, a decision reached. "A staff member," he declared flatly. "Most likely, ex-staff."

I studied the list of names. "Did you sleep with everyone on the list?" I finally asked.

"Only the first eight," he replied. It wasn't very helpful, however, since there were ten names listed. I struggled to hide my repulsion. I could not imagine getting intimate with this doughy man!

"Okay, I'll get started on this list. By the way, I brought you something." I held up the plastic bag I'd been holding. "Since we've partnered, I believe you now realize that I have no vested interest in harming you, so I took the liberty of packing you some food from the bistro." His eyes shone as he grabbed the bag.

"Thank you, Missy. Much appreciated. Please stay in touch with updates." With that, he held the bag of food to his chest like a newborn then ushered me out the door and closed it behind me. I shrugged, tucked the list of names into my purse and headed home to create a plan of action.

I curled up on the couch with a cup of coffee and perused the list. He'd been surprisingly thorough and the list was well organized. I zeroed in on the list of ex-staff members. Jenny Rathwell, 24. Megan Miller, 22. Elizabeth Wagner, 21. Elvira Zander, 22. The list continued along the same vein and I shook my head, bewildered that such young women had tangoed with the Toad. Were they all hoping for a sugar daddy?

I decided to start with the first couple of ex-staff members, then a couple of the people from the "business acquaintances" list. I should easily get to a minimum of four people the next day. I googled the directions to all of their addresses, mapped out my itinerary for the next day, and then pranced off to get ready for my date with Nathan.

After a long, steamy shower, I took my time drying and styling my hair then stood in front of the fan to cool off before donning yellow undies and bra and then my pale yellow dress. I gave my eye-makeup a final smudge for a softer look, fluffed my hair a final time then downed a glass of wine to calm my nerves. Smacking my lips in appreciation, I poured another glass of Lucky Night and forced myself to sit still and sip it. That lasted all of fifteen seconds before I downed that glass too, and then paced about, waiting for the knock at my door. It finally came at ten minutes to three and I put on a sexy smile and flung the door open.

There stood Hans with a stunned expression on his face. He took in the long gown and then snapped his gaping jaw shut so quickly that I could hear his teeth clack. My own smile froze and turned into a sneer. "What now?" I asked bluntly. He worked his lips like a fish out of water, but no sound came forth. Finally, he burbled "Why did you have to leave me?" and then bounded down the stairs and back to his car. I stared in surprise and horror. Where had that come from? In his haste to peel out of my driveway, his tires spun and he nicked the front left bumper of a Jeep that was turning into my lot. I continued to stare in horror as Nathan got out of the Jeep, inspected his bumper then waved a cheery greeting to Hans, who then drove away. Apparently, no harm was done and Nathan was as gracious as he was handsome. Climbing back into the Jeep, he glanced my way and froze. Even from a distance, I was pretty sure I could make out the expression, "Wow!" He parked his car and bounded up the stairs.

He stopped just millimeters from me, our lips almost touching, the electricity practically crackling between us. A bright smile lit his face and his eyes shone. "Hi," he whispered gently, before finally making contact. The kiss was as tender as a feather dancing across my lips. I kissed back, just as gently, savoring the feeling, unrushed. When we broke apart, our eyes met in wonder.

"Wow," he whispered, just as he'd done the day before. I nodded, not trusting myself to speak. It was a wow moment indeed, and the electricity that was created in that one little kiss was wondrous.

"Um, is your Jeep okay?" I ended up blurting out, too afraid of what else might come out of my mouth after that amazing kiss.

"Not a scratch. Do you know the person that was spitting gravel?"

I cringed. "Oh, yes. That was my ex from a couple of years back." His brows rose in surprise. "He comes by every now and then to torment me. I have no clue what he might have wanted tonight. He left without saying much."

Nathan looked a bit troubled. "Should I be worrying about this guy?" he asked. I could almost visualize an invisible wall slowly going up between us.

My response was a hearty laugh. "Absolutely not! Now, shall we enjoy our date? The last thing I want to do is waste our time talking about him!"

He offered his arm to me as we walked down the stairs together. At the bottom he pulled me to him for another soft kiss that ended with hard breathing. "We better get going," he said, giving me a long glance from head to toe. "The wine tasting starts soon, I'm sure you don't want to miss it."

"Wine tasting? What a good idea! Where are we going?"

"Nicastros Botega, downtown. It's a delicatessen but they also have wine and cheese paring sessions to help promote the cheeses that they sell. I thought it would be fun, and after that, maybe we can go for a walk around the market area before choosing a restaurant for dinner." He beamed at me, clearly pleased with his choice of plans for the evening.

"An excellent idea," I concurred.

Six glasses of wine and six varieties of cheeses later, we half-stumbled out of Nicastros. "I can't believe how much wine they gave us," he said, blinking to bring me into focus. "I thought it would be a mouthful of each—those glasses were almost full!"

I giggled in response. "I'm glad I took notes, because I can't remember anything we learnt right now. Some of it is bound to be useful for my line of work. Shall we *attempt* to walk around the market?"

"I have a better idea. Let's try to find some coffee first," he suggested, and I nodded enthusiastically. We zipped into the first coffee shop we found and downed the coffees in record time while slowly walking around the Byward Market, a section of Ottawa known for its restaurants and outdoor market area. Here one could buy fresh fruit and vegetables, handmade trinkets, go to the European deli and stock up on salamis or visit one of the many bars and restaurants, all within a few blocks.

"Are you in the mood for anything particular for dinner?" he asked.

"To be honest, I'm not even hungry! After all that bread, cheese and the six glasses of wine, I can't even imagine putting anything else into my stomach," I moaned. He grinned then reached out to tuck my hair behind my ear.

"You're absolutely beautiful," he murmured gently, before giving me another of his feather light kisses. My stomach chose that moment to begin digesting and a garbled sound travelled up my esophagus, much to my embarrassment.

"Pardon me!" I exclaimed, mortified. "That sound actually came from my stomach," I clarified, in case there was any doubt, then started giggling uncontrollably. His eyes had widened in surprise and soon we were both howling with laughter.

"I have an idea," I finally said, gulping for air and wiping tears from my eyes. "What I'd really like to do is simply get to know you better. Would you like to come back to the bistro for more coffee or drinks? And if we get hungry later, we can whip up something."

He smiled sweetly. "I'd love that." Grabbing my hand, he led me back to his Jeep and opened the door for me before heading to the driver's side.

Half an hour later, we were settled by the fire in the bistro, sharing a nice bottle of Pinot Noire called Swoon.

"I honestly didn't think I could drink any more wine tonight, but I was obviously wrong," Nathan joked, while taking a long, appreciative sip and shifting closer to me on the couch, then taking my free hand in his.

We remained there for the next few hours, exchanging stories of our past and dreams for our futures, interrupted only by brief, and not so brief, periods of kissing. Near midnight, he exhaled a huge sigh and reluctantly got to his feet. "I'd love to be here all night, but I have to be up in a few hours to work." He looked at me sadly. "Will you be free again tomorrow night?" he asked hopefully.

My face lit up like fireworks. "Absolutely!" I replied, confident that my investigations for the day would be wrapped up by that time.

"How about seven o'clock?" I nodded enthusiastically until he grabbed my cheeks gently and gave me a deep kiss and then a devilish smile. "Until tomorrow, then." A last caress from his tongue, and he was gone, leaving me stunned from the emotions coursing through me.

"I'm doomed," I whispered aloud to no one. He was everything my previous ex's weren't, and everything that I'd been looking for, but didn't dare to hope for. My loins lurched again, reminding me they existed. "Yeah, yeah, I hear you," I grumbled.

I floated on my cloud, straightening the bistro before retiring to my living quarters. Hummer greeted me at the door, squinting at me in disgust. I had forgotten to give him the moist, smelly food that he normally received, and he was not pleased. Plus, he sensed that I had met someone special. *Wipe that silly smile off your face,* I could almost hear him saying. I set about preparing his dish and life was good again.

Chapter Nineteen

I opened my eyes to find Hummer wearing his infamous look of disgust. Our eyes locked in a stare-down, but he won. He usually does.

"Oh stop it," I grumbled, my good humor dissipating as his stinky cat breath brought me fully awake. He barked (I swear) and jumped off my bed, his tail quivering his opinion of our morning exchange. Or perhaps he found my human breath equally repulsive.

With substantial effort, I shook thoughts of Nathan aside long enough to get dressed and fill my body with caffeine while mentally organizing my plans for the day. I carefully laid out the route I would take to interview the various suspects. I wasn't a cop or a private investigator, so why would anyone speak frankly with me?

An idea formed. Of course! I would simply say that I'm working on the investigation for Milton. I wouldn't be lying, and they would probably assume that I have some type of investigative credentials. Brilliant! Then I frowned, remembering that one of these people might be a murderer. I needed backup. But who would play the role?

I picked up my cell phone, took a deep breath and placed a call. Luckily, my dad answered, and after exchanging pleasantries, and confirming for the two thousandth time that I was not interested in taking accounting classes, I pitched my idea to him as best I could in my broken Hungarian, and he readily agreed. He'd recuperated nicely from his previous jitters and was eager to be my snooping sidekick. I told him to wear something business-like and hoped for the best.

He showed up raring to go, dressed in his classic brown pants and yellow, polyester shirt. I groaned inwardly, but I was not surprised. What excuse he gave my mother for his impromptu outing, I have yet to find out. When questioned, he smiled coyly and told me not to worry about her.

We arrived at the home of the first suspect and were lucky enough to catch her on her way inside. Jenny Rathwell was a perky blonde that filled her clothes nicely. For the life of me, I could not fathom what she saw in Milton.

She readily bought my story that we both were hired by Milton to aid in the investigation of the death of his wife, and looked genuinely saddened when discussing Blanche's death.

"Ms. Rathwell, Milton indicated to me that you had a relationship with him outside the roles of employer and employee. Is that correct?"

She blushed deeply. "Yes," she mumbled, lowering

her eyes. "I'm not proud of it. I was putting myself through college and he offered to help me pay. It didn't last long. I simply couldn't…continue." She shuddered as she placed a hand against her mouth, as if she were repulsed.

"A pretty voman like you? Son of a gun!" my dad blurted. I glared at him and he quickly wiped the smirk off his face.

"Did it end badly?" I prodded.

She finally met my eyes and gave me a meek look "If he hired you, you must already know what happened."

"Actually, he didn't give me specifics. I take it things did not end amicably."

She sighed deeply. "I had a boyfriend at the time. I was in love with him. Milton threatened to tell him about our relationship if I left. I stayed another month, but after catching my boyfriend with another woman, I figured I had nothing to lose, so I found the courage to leave."

"Did Milton ever tell your boyfriend?"

"Ex-boyfriend," she corrected. "No, he never did, but after catching him cheating on me, and not feeling proud of myself for what I'd done, the relationship ended, so it didn't matter anymore."

"When was the last time you saw Milton or Blanche?"

"The day I quit, which was probably about a year ago," she said simply.

"Do you recall where you were the night Blanche died?" I tried to sound nonchalant.

"So that's where all this is leading…" She laughed

nervously. "I don't know if I should be flattered or insulted. Either way, I work as a nanny now and had to accompany the family I work for to Florida during their vacation to take care of the kids, and I haven't even been here for more than a month, so it wasn't me. Will there be anything else?"

Satisfied, I thanked her for talking to us and my dad offered a final smirk until I subtly kicked him in the shin. What had gotten into him?

As we drove to the home of the next suspect, he admitted he was surprised that Milton could land someone so young and attractive. I mentioned that the next suspect we were seeing would likely be the same and for him to keep his cool and remain quiet. He was merely my barrel-chested, scrawny-armed, chicken-legged muscle man in case something went wrong, plus he looked fairly fragile, so people would likely be less intimidated with him at my side.

After speaking with Megan Miller, who also had an air-tight alibi, we were no further along. As both interviews were over quickly, I decided to try the third girl on the list, Elizabeth Wagner. Despite knocking on her door, ringing the bell, and nonchalantly glancing through her accessible windows, no one stirred within. I made a note to try her again at a different time the next day.

Next on my list were the Gregsons, and I was not looking forward to it. Would they recognize me from the bistro? We pulled up in front of their house, a three-story brick home with a wrap-around veranda

and a large, manicured yard. Mrs. Gregson herself
answered the door; no maids or servants here. She
looked at me questioningly, though without a sign
of recognition. Once I offered my story that I was
investigating the case privately for Milton, and intro-
duced my brown and yellow "associate", she let us
inside and led us to the living room.

"Please, sit. May I bring you some coffee?" I
politely declined for both of us, sensing my dad was
going to say yes. I wasn't going to take the chance of
drinking something that had been poisoned.

"Is Mr. Gregson at home?" I inquired politely.

"No, he's at work, but I'm more than happy
to answer whatever questions you might have. If
you'd like to speak with him afterward, I would
suggest booking an appointment at his office since
he's been keeping very long hours lately." She let
out a small sigh, and then continued softly, "I'm
still sad about Blanche's death. She was a very dear
friend, you know."

I nodded sympathetically. "Yes, Milton mentioned
that you were close and thought that perhaps she
might have confided in you. Did she ever indicate
that someone was after her?"

"No, not her. But him? Anyone and everyone. It
would certainly have made sense if he'd been the one
to drop dead, not that I wish him harm, of course.
But Blanche was a genuinely nice person. I saw her
just days before her death at a luncheon. She did
not appear to be under stress; she was smiling and

joking like always. A touch pale, perhaps, but that might just be my imagination playing tricks on me now. We saw her briefly that day, too, of course. We had been at the bistro and Greg had stopped for a word with Milton." Her voice faded as she looked deep in thought.

When she didn't continue after several moments, I gently asked, "Was there anything unusual about that day?" She blinked, clearing her watery eyes.

"It's no secret that Greg and Milton exchanged unfriendly words. The police are aware of it, of course, and to be honest, it was just the usual banter any time they came face to face in a social setting. So, in answer to your question, no, there was nothing unusual."

I tried a different tactic: "Did the unfriendly exchange include Blanche?"

"No, of course not; we were both very fond of Blanche."

To that, I tried to put on a stern face, very difficult for me as I'm usually quite cheerful. "Milton did hint at a history between your husband and Blanche. Would there be any truth to that?" She diverted her eyes. A stab of guilt ran through me. I was not cut out to play the "bad cop" role.

"Yes, it's true," she replied, her voice barely above a whisper. "It is so embarrassing, discussing this with a stranger. They dated briefly before Blanche met Milton, but then Greg and I met shortly after and fell in love. He never gave her a second thought after that."

"Do I understand correctly that you and Blanche used to *work* together?" I asked, more softly this time. Lea blushed deeply again.

"I assume all of this will be kept strictly confidential. I'm a very respectable woman. I make no secret of my past, but it certainly wouldn't be beneficial to dredge it up now. Yes, we worked together briefly. When Greg and I started dating, I quit working at the escort service almost immediately." She averted her eyes, and I picked up on her wording. *Almost* immediately...

She fixed her eyes on me, her lips now pursed. "We were not exclusive at first. But as things became more serious, and I was swept away by his charm, I made a mistake. I forgot to take my birth control and ended up pregnant. So I quit the escort service and moved in with Greg. Sadly, we lost the baby. We were both devastated, but during the three months that I was carrying, our love grew strong and remains strong to this day. But I doubt that any of this is relevant, Ms. Kis."

"I agree, Mrs. Gregson. And I'm so sorry. However, I would like to speak to Mr. Gregson too, if you would ask him to call me?" Without thinking, I slipped her my business card for the Whine and Cheese and only realized my error when her eyes widened in surprise.

"I'm sure I don't understand what's going on here, but you're going to explain now, aren't you, Ms. Kis?" It wasn't so much a question as a statement. I nodded.

"I understand your confusion. What I said when I arrived was the truth. I am investigating the case for Milton, and as the owner of the bistro, I have the added concern of clearing my name. I have been involved in some cases in the past, successfully, I may add, so rest assured that I do have some investigative experience and will naturally keep everything we discussed confidential."

She looked at me pensively before speaking. "Having you investigate this case would be a conflict of interest, Ms. Kis. How do I know that you're not trying to find out just enough information to pin the murder on us? I'm afraid that this interview is now over. I'm not sure just who this rather odd looking gentleman with you might be, but I'm sure that you can both find your way out." She rose to signal the end of the conversation.

"Thank you for your time," I mumbled, as my dad and I hurried to the door.

Once safely inside the car and on our way back to the bistro, my dad asked, "Vat she say, I look funny?" He sounded offended or even hurt, and a corner of my lip twitched.

"I'm not sure, Dad. At that point I was in a hurry to get out of there, so I didn't quite hear her. I'm sure she said no such thing. I mean, look at you! I'm sure she said something about how snazzy you're dressed." He beamed with pride over my small fib, quickly accepting what I said because that was what he wished to believe, or perhaps truly did believe.

"Okay, so here's my interpretation of what she told us. Blanche had been Greg's escort, until Milton came along, and for some reason, she fell in love with him. At that point, Greg took Lea as his escort. She began to have feelings for him but knew he still had a thing for Blanche, therefore she did what so many women have done in the past: she either got pregnant, and lost the baby, or lied about being pregnant. During the "pregnancy", Greg developed feelings for her and was finally able to put thoughts of Blanche aside, although he still carried a torch for her. What do you think, Dad?"

He agreed that it all sounded logical, adding only that perhaps Greg stayed with Lea out of guilt after the loss of the baby. Still, I wondered why she had shared the story with us. Was it simply to draw us a picture of their love for each other, or to vanquish any thought that Greg was still interested in Blanche? If anything, it only made me more suspicious.

"Thanks for coming with me. Do you think you can come again tomorrow?" I asked hopefully, pulling up next to his car in my parking lot. He declined, explaining that he wouldn't be able to escape my mother two days in a row without arousing suspicion, but did promise to try to come over later that week to discuss the case and my findings.

With nothing more left on the agenda, I was free to prepare for my date with Nathan. Finally allowing myself the luxury of thinking about him, my veins buzzed as my temperature rose. He'd texted me quickly earlier in the day, just to tell me to dress casual. Other than that, I had no clue what to expect. I was just about to step into the shower when my phone vibrated with an unknown caller. I hesitated, then at the last moment, decided to answer. I regretted it immediately.

Chapter Twenty

"Ms. Kis?" The male caller barked at me.

"I, uh, yes, I think so," I mumbled in surprise as the man's hostility roiled over the phone lines like a tidal wave.

"This is Greg Gregson. I understand you spoke with my wife today and requested to speak with me as well. If you ever approach either of us again, Ms. Kis, I will personally see to it that your life becomes very unpleasant. We have nothing further to say unless someone with official credentials comes to see us. We have already been extremely co-operative and we do not appreciate this intrusion into our lives. Am I clear, Ms. Kis?"

"Of course, Mr. Gregson," I mumbled timidly, hating that I had nothing witty to say or any official credentials to back me up. Before I could offer an explanation or an apology, he hung up on me.

Feeling dejected, I decided to draw a relaxing bath rather than have a shower, and I poured myself a tall glass of Rough Day. Pouring in extra bubble bath liquid, I sank into the water and watched the bubbles grow around me. I felt instantly calmer. A few healthy sips of the white wine further relaxed me, as did the heat of the water. Soon, my ego was on the mend.

Of course, Mr. and Mrs. Gregson had every right to be upset with me. They no doubt both thought that Milton and I had teamed up to pin Blanche's murder on them, just as Mrs. Gregson had indicated. With the bad history between them, I was lucky that Greg had actually been as polite as he was with me. I had been stupid to give Lea my business card, so I had only myself to blame, and if I intended to continue with the investigation, I knew that I had better develop a tougher skin.

Hummer jumped onto the ledge of the bathtub to console me. He gave me a sympathetic look, and then reached down with a furry paw to bat at the bubbles. His antics further lightened my mood and I was soon in good spirits again, ready to prepare for my date with Nathan.

Dragging my body out of the water, I patted myself dry with a fluffy towel then slathered my body from head to toe with lotion, followed by a few sprays of my new favorite scent, Bombshell. Next, I dried and styled my hair and reapplied makeup. Donning a pair of form-fitting jeans and a white, flowy, sleeveless top, I was ready and had just a few minutes to spare. Right on time, Nathan's knock sounded at the door. Hummer growled menacingly as I grinned ear to ear.

Opening the door, I was suddenly shy, but still

wore the giant grin on my face. To my relief, he wore an identical grin as he pulled me into his embrace, enveloping me in his warmth, strength and scent. I breathed deeply; the smell of sun and love and life, if such a thing could be bottled and recreated. Reluctantly, he loosened his hold but didn't let go. "You might need a light sweater, but it's still warm out so we'll be okay for a while."

"Where are we going?" I asked, not trusting myself to say too much as I was still wrapped in his delicious scent. He grinned even wider.

"Not far at all. In fact, we don't even have to take the car. And you won't need your purse either," he said, as I reached for it. I began to get nervous. The only place close enough to have dinner other than my bistro was Leonardo's. How could I explain to Nathan that I couldn't set foot in that place without embarrassing myself?

But I needn't have worried. As we got to the base of my stairs, I saw a beautiful picnic basket, on top of which lay a blanket. He stopped to retrieve both in one hand, then used the other to firmly grasp my hand and gently tug me toward my backyard.

The sun was still shining brightly and the warmth made me grin even wider as I helped Nathan lay the blanket amongst my beautiful, poisonous plants. We both sat and then he began unloading the goodies from within the picnic basket. Two wine glasses, a sourdough baguette, a couple of different cheeses, some fried chicken and a bottle of red wine. He had removed the label and created his own, having drawn a heart and the words "Perfect Date' onto a blank piece of paper which he'd cut down to the size of a label and glued to the bottle. My cheeks were beginning to hurt from smiling so widely and I feared that my face would soon split.

We munched and talked and snuggled until the sun began to set and the temperature dropped. Although it was a perfect date, I couldn't shake the sense of being watched, since we were out in the open. More than a few times, I glanced in the direction of the hiking trails. Could someone be hidden amongst the trees, watching us? Eli, perhaps, who kept crossing my path unexpectedly? Or the blonde who'd tried to run over Milton?

As the spring air became too cold to comfortably sit outside, we packed the leftovers into the basket. I asked if he wanted to come inside for a cup of coffee and to warm up by the fireplace in the bistro, and we did just that, and talked until well past midnight although it felt like only minutes had passed.

"Where does the time go?" he murmured into my ear, giving me a final goodnight hug and kiss. "You've made an incredible impact in the past few days. My lips ache for yours when we're apart. I don't even begin to try to understand it, after such a short time knowing you."

I was speechless. Never had I heard such beautiful words—not said to me, anyway! "I…I feel the same," I barely whispered, afraid to make the admission and bewildered by these strange and sudden emotions. More final kisses followed until he managed to pry himself away. He promised to call me the next day.

I tidied up the already impeccable bistro to burn off energy and to try to organize my thoughts. I couldn't help but compare my time with Nathan to my time with Matt. Although I had felt excited and stimulated by Matt, with Nathan it was just so much more. Perhaps it was because we'd already spent so much more time just talking and getting to know each other, whereas my time with Matt always seemed to be stolen hours here and there in between finding bodies and his assignments that always took him away. Whatever it was, I knew that this time I had found something rare, assuming that Nathan was genuine. Was it too perfect to be true?

The next morning, I awoke with the same goofy smile still on my face. "Damn, at this rate, I'll be wrinkled from smiling within a few years!" I exclaimed to Hummer, who really didn't care. I groused anyway, as he continued to ignore me.

I quickly planned my day. I wanted another attempt at Elizabeth Wagner's house, so I thought I'd go there first, then I would have to meet with Milton to report my findings to date. There'd be little time for much else though as I had to do my weekly cheese and salami purchases and make a trip for fresh bread. Truth be told, I was also quite dispirited after the call from Mr. Gregson and was not looking forward to admitting my blunder to Milton.

I called Beth, hoping for a back-up partner. She declined, claiming to have plans. I resigned myself to the fact that I was on my own for the day and that I'd have to be extra careful.

Dressed, fed, caffeinated and therefore slightly invigorated, I returned to the home of the illusive Elizabeth. This time, there was a black car in the driveway, and I felt a spike of excitement. Still trying to work up the nerve to interrogate someone after the lecture from Mr. Gregson, I hesitated and instead parked my car across the street and one door down, allowing me a clear line of vision to Elizabeth's place. In case anyone came sniffing around, I quickly took out an area map. I needed to pretend that I was lost, and I held my phone to my ear, as though in conversation.

I watched intently for five minutes, quickly tiring of the stakeout, and then impatiently reached for the door handle, my mind made up. "I'm going in," I said aloud, but before I could pull the handle, Elizabeth's door suddenly opened and a woman with long, flowing blonde hair emerged and hurried to her car. Watching her move, something about her seemed familiar, but yet, I knew I had never seen her before. Although I was not a fan of blonde hair, hers was stunning. I could imagine men swooning at her feet. Certainly, Milton would have...

I came out of my trance long enough to start my car, preparing for pursuit. This was something I'd done before, and thoroughly enjoyed the chase. I gave her a ten second head start, not daring to wait any longer in case I lost her. With my eyes on my prey, I followed at a safe distance. With each passing mile, my trepidation grew. By the time we neared Milton's house, I was sweating profusely, on high alert, knowing it wasn't a coincidence. I tried to reason with myself; she'd worked here before, therefore she'd likely made some friends in the area. Mind you, she had been hired help. Was hired help allowed to socialize in the neighborhood?

She drove past Milton's house slowly. Not wanting to risk getting caught, I pulled over and parked on the road, letting her move further ahead. Without warning, she quickly pulled a U-turn, and before I knew it, she was driving past my car as I hunkered down, not wanting to be spotted. I stayed in that position for several minutes before daring to poke my head up for a look. To my relief, she was nowhere in sight, and I was too shaken to try to find her.

Regaining my composure, I pulled onto the shoulder of the road at the bottom of Milton's driveway. I walked towards the house slowly, not looking forward to having to report my findings, and more specifically, my blunder.

Chapter Twenty-One

The door flew open and I braced myself. "Missy!" He glanced about. "Where's the food?" He looked crestfallen.

"I'm sorry Milton. I was following Elizabeth Wagner, and to my shock, she led me here. Since I was just steps away, I figured I'd come to see you first. I can send someone over with the food, if you like, or you can…" He cut me off before I could finish.

"Oh no, I'll come to get it myself. Other than you, I trust no one. Now, what do you mean, she came here? Come in, for heaven's sake; why are you still standing out there? Now, tell me everything," he commanded once he sat me down upon a couch so plush that it practically swallowed me whole.

"Well," I murmured from deep within the cushions, "I was staking out her place and…" I was interrupted by the ringing of my phone. I reached for the button to dismiss the call but accidentally hit the answer button.

"Hello, is this Syrah?" a sugary voice asked. Hot damn! The escort agency was calling me for an interview, at the worst time imaginable.

"Yes, this is she," I replied, trying to sound casual.

"Madame LaJambe has an opening tomorrow morning and has requested that you join her for a meeting. May I tell her to expect you?"

"Oh, yes, absolutely," I said while trying to regain my composure. "I would appreciate that." I confirmed the time then hung up, offering my apologies to Milton but hurrying to explain that it was in relation to the investigation. "I can't share more information about it yet, but soon." He scowled but his features quickly softened as I filled him in on my findings over the last couple of days.

In a weak attempt to stall before outlining my encounter with the Gregsons, I allowed myself a moment to backtrack to the reason I had arrived so early. "Before I continue, Milton, would you have a clue why Elizabeth would be coming to this area? She slowed as she passed your home but then did an abrupt U-turn and sped away."

"She's probably the murderer and came back to kill me but got cold feet. She'd have no other reason to come here." He answered far too calmly, seemingly not alarmed by her presence in the area.

"Can you describe her to me, so I can make sure that we're talking about the same person?" He described her perfectly, dwelling mainly on her gorgeous head of hair. I did not want to know what he was remembering to prompt his smile.

"How, or why, did things end with her? And do

you recall when?" I whipped out my trusty notepad and began scribbling as he spoke.

"It seemed to be going well. She had been here quite a while, so we'd developed quite a bond, you see. One day, she seemed to get mad at me for no reason, and our little arrangement abruptly ended. She quit working for me shortly after that. That was about two months ago."

"Maybe she wanted to give her condolences about Blanche. And maybe she was just trying to gather the courage to speak to you…"

He shrugged in response. "It's a mystery. It's not like we actually fought, and she got along well with Blanche."

"Do you happen to recall what your last words to her were?" I knew it was a long shot, but Milton surprised me.

"Yes, I do. It was about salad, of all things. She was our housekeeper but would also fill in for the cook at times. I had asked her to prepare a salad that day. Blanche had had me on a fairly strict diet for months, and I actually found myself starting to enjoy salads."

"Salad?" I repeated, feeling a stab of alarm. Blanche had been poisoned via the salad she'd eaten, which had originally been served to Milton. "Did she seem mad after that?"

"I don't recall. I was engrossed in my computer at the time, doing some number crunching for a client. I believe that's the last I saw of her, though."

I racked my brain, trying to remember if I had

seen her at the bistro before, in particular on that day. But of course, if I had seen her, I would have remembered her and her positively luscious hair, and Milton and Blanche would surely have noticed her. In fact, anyone within her vicinity would have noticed her. I put it on the backburner for the time being, squared my shoulders, and briefed Milton on my visit with Mrs. Gregson. As I explained the business card blunder, I could feel my cheeks warming with embarrassment and my stomach knotting.

To my surprise, he laughed heartily, clearly not the reaction I'd expected. I wasn't sure if I should say something or quietly slink away. Before I could decide, he put me out of my misery.

"Oh, that's priceless, Missy. I can just imagine the looks on their faces. No doubt they're feeling the pressure now. I'm still certain that Greg has something to do with it. I just can't shake that feeling. Maybe it's just because I'd love to see him behind bars. No harm, Missy."

I breathed a sigh of relief and began to take my leave. "I'll prepare a platter for you as soon as I get back to the bistro, so it'll be ready whenever you're able to stop by," I promised. He licked his lips as I stepped into the sunshine. Making my way down the driveway to my car, I breathed a sigh of relief that he'd found my blunder amusing.

As I drove away, I glanced uneasily in the direction of Eli-the-drug-dealer's house. My blood froze in my veins when I spotted a black car in the driveway. Was it Elizabeth's car? Could that have been the purpose of her trip here? If so, why the slow cruise past Milton's house? Was she a drug addict? Could that be the reason for her relationship with Milton? I had to find out if he gave his lovers extra spending money. And why, oh why, had I not noticed her plate number?

I pulled over quickly and turned the car around, driving by Eli's home at a crawl, trying to get a glimpse at the license plate number. Damn these long driveways—it was just too far for me to be able to clearly make it out. Giving up, I sped home, fixed Milton a platter of food, took stock of what I needed, then headed out to run my errands.

Truth be told, this was my favorite day of the week, the day that the bistro's cheeses and salamis were restocked. I made the twenty-minute trek to Serious Cheese in the west end of Ottawa, my mouth watering in anticipation.

I picked up some pre-made pizza dough, made in-house, for taste-testing purposes. It could be a future item on the menu if I could come up with something original. I began to envision a cheese and salami pizza and my mouth watered uncontrollably. Next, the cheese section, where a horseradish mozzarella caught my eye. That was original! I'd have to give it a try, as well as the roasted garlic mozzarella and some creamy, low sodium feta. I loaded my basket with a number of other cheeses, took a few minutes to eat a wonderful grilled cheese sandwich, and then made my way downtown to La Bottega Nicastro for deli meats, where Nate and I had gone for the wine and cheese tasting the other day.

I stocked up on Italian prosciutto, Soppressata, Genoa, and Hungarian salamis, some Mortadella and a dozen other mouthwatering choices. My last stop was the Rideau Bakery for an assortment of breads. While I had a wholesale arrangement with them, I still enjoyed the weekly in-person trip. This time, I chose a few loaves of rye, pumpernickel, French and Italian breads then rushed back to the bistro to prepare for opening.

After the delicious grilled cheese sandwich that I'd just eaten, I knew I had to serve something similar as tonight's featured item. It would be nicely complimented with a small bowl of ham and potato chowder, and I'd make the grilled sandwiches with a mixture of three cheeses.

To my surprise, Billy walked in, considerably early for his shift, and offered to help. While I mixed ingredients and set the soup to simmer, Billy paired some garlic Havarti, Swiss and Emmental cheese slices together and separated each grouping with a sheet of plastic wrap. These would be used in the three-cheese grilled sandwiches, and having them pre-organized would speed up the process once the orders were placed. Last but not least, we began preparing the deli meat and cheese platters for the night. All that would be left would be to add a handful of nuts, grapes and olives, as well as bread or crackers, once the customers placed their orders. Topped off with a drizzle of olive oil and a sprinkling of chopped rosemary, cilantro, chives and fresh parsley from my little herb garden, it would be mouthwatering.

As we were finishing, he casually asked if Beth would be working that evening and looked dejected when I replied that she would not. So that was the reason he'd arrived so early! I looked at him slyly before commenting that Chloé, however, would be present. He politely muttered, "Oh, that's nice," before shuffling away. It seemed his crush on her had officially been replaced with one on Beth; nevertheless, I was pleased that Billy was starting to come out of his shell.

I checked the time and was surprised to see that there was still half an hour before opening time. In the midst of pouring myself a glass of wine, and already mentally savoring it, I was startled by the sudden loud banging on my back door. It flew open to reveal Milton looking quite frazzled.

One of these days, I may actually remember to lock that door.

Supreme Grilled Cheese

Not everything in life has to be complicated and that includes supper time.

- 2 thick slices of bread (such as a Texas-Toast sandwich bread)
- 3 cheeses of your choice (such as Havarti, Emmental, Swiss, Gouda, sliced bocconcini, mozzarella, cheddar – let your imagination run wild, throw in a little feta or goat cheese)
- Margarine or cooking spray or mayonnaise (not miracle whip)

Healthier version: spray the outside of each side of bread with cooking spray

Less healthy version: coat the outside of each slice of bread with a thin, even layer of margarine or use mayonnaise for an extra little dash of flavor. Trust me, it grills nicely.

Assemble the cheese between the two slices of bread and place sandwich in frying pan over medium heat. Wait a few minutes before gently checking the bottom of the sandwich to see if it's nicely toasted. If not, patiently wait another minute or two, gently checking constantly. Once nicely grilled, flip gently until the other side of the sandwich is equally grilled.

Place on plate, slice in half and serve with a dollop of ketchup on the side for dipping.

Chapter Twenty-Two

I stopped in mid-pour, taking note of his disheveled hair and frantic expression. "What happened?" I whispered, not daring to move a muscle.

"Someone tried to ram into my car!" he gasped, his eyes bulging.

"Where?" I asked, thinking that the driver might have followed him right to my door. I was shocked to find out that I wasn't far off.

"On the road right in front of the bistro. The car suddenly appeared on my tail; we were just about to make contact when I gunned the engine then quickly turned into your parking lot." His words tumbled from him in one breath, leaving him gasping.

"Did you get a look at the car? Was it black?" I was on pins and needles, wondering if it was Elizabeth.

He shook his head "It happened so fast, I couldn't tell. I think it was a dark car, possibly black, but I can't say for certain. There appeared to be two people in it. But I could be wrong about that too. You know, Greg drives a black car, too. Maybe it was him and

Lea. I wouldn't put it past that scoundrel."

"Two?" I was stumped. "I suppose it could just be a coincidence, some kids joy-riding perhaps, or possibly Greg and Lea but my instinct tells me it's not them." Two people... I thought I'd had the case figured out, but this twist threw a wrench into the machinery. Perhaps Milton was wrong about two people riding in the car.

His breathing calmed and I caught him glancing at the fridge. "Let me get your platter, Milton. Do you want to sit here and relax awhile?" I set him up in my office with his platter and an uncorked bottle of wine. I heard him sigh with contentment as I hurried away to open the bistro for the customers.

I checked on him again about fifteen minutes later, as he was finishing his meat. He snorted at my suggestion to call the police, dismissing it wordlessly. I took advantage of this unexpected time with him and posed the question I had thought of earlier.

"Milton, I need to ask you a delicate question, for the investigation. The people with whom you had relations: did you give them money or gifts as incentive, or in appreciation for their services?" I bumbled my way through, hoping he wouldn't be too insulted.

"Well, I suppose so. If it was an extended relationship, I'd give them extra spending money sometimes. Why do you ask?"

"Just a question that occurred to me; nothing I can put my finger on just yet." I didn't want to hurt his feelings by telling him that I couldn't understand what the women possibly saw in him. Clearly, his extracurricular lovers had adequate incentive to sleep with him.

I was thankful that the remainder of the evening was uneventful, and around midnight, Chloé, Nicole and I settled down with our usual post-work glass of wine. Billy declined an invitation to join us and headed home, a leftover grilled cheese sandwich in hand.

"How was your date with Dashing Drew?" I asked Nicole, not having heard any details as of yet and dying to find out. She had coyly averted my questions all night long, allowing only a smirk in response.

"Scrumptious," she sighed, then took a long swallow of wine, her eyes closed and a smile playing on her lips.

"Do you mean Drew was scrumptious?" Chloé prompted, her eyes glowing in anticipation.

"Oh, that too," Nicole giggled. "We went to a quiet little bistro downtown and spent a couple of hours lingering over our food and drinks, then to another quaint restaurant and had coffee with Baileys Irish Cream liquor while sitting on the patio. The conversation flowed so naturally. I like him," she stated, though she was frowning.

"So why do you look so troubled?" I questioned.

"You know what happened the last time I liked someone." It hadn't ended well for Nicole, nor had many of the countless dates that she'd had in recent years.

"Quit overthinking things," I chided. "Just let it

happen naturally. If it doesn't come naturally, then you're with the wrong person. And you said the conversation came naturally, so that's a good start."

She nodded and was about to respond when Nora flew into the room in a tizzy.

"Thank God you're all still here!" She sank onto a chair, grabbed the wine and drank straight from the bottle. "Oh, don't give me that look, there's hardly anything left in here," she snarled, and then turned sweet as sherry the next moment.

"I can't believe someone tried to off Milton," she gossiped.

I knew I hadn't mentioned the incident, nor had I really analyzed recent events. "He's fine," I assured. "When he first showed up, he was pretty jumpy. It seems that someone, possibly two people in one car, tried to run him off the road right in front of the bistro. He'd made it here safely, but of course the incident has him convinced that someone is out to kill him."

Possibly me too, I thought to myself.

"I don't believe that Blanche was ever the intended victim, since Milton had switched salads with her. I had gone to interview a suspect earlier today, but instead ended up following her to Milton's house. Then she made an abrupt U-Turn and ended up at Eli the Drug Dealer's house, I think. I wasn't completely certain that it was her car, but it was a black vehicle like the one I'd followed. Milton isn't sure what kind of car tried to run him off the road, but he was pretty sure that it was dark—possibly black. How did you hear about it, Nora?" As if I didn't already know.

"Someone at Leonardo's mentioned it when I was at the cash register. They saw the entire incident while driving to Leo's but said it all happened so fast that they didn't have a chance to get a good look at the car before it sped off. They did recognize Milton's car though, and saw him pull in here. Leonardo almost kicked them out just for mentioning the bistro's name!" She giggled and polished off the last of the wine in the bottle with a smack of her lips.

I couldn't help but smile as her laugh was infectious. "Alright gang, time to call it a night. I have an important meeting tomorrow morning with Madame LaJambe."

Their eyebrows rose at the name. "Yes, she's quite tall," I answered their unspoken question. In French, la jambe means the leg. "She's also the Madame for the escort agency where Blanche worked. I went there posing as an applicant to get some information about Blanche, but I still have questions. I'm not sure if there's anything more I might learn, but I'm going to try. I've had to wait for Madame to be available to interview me, while in fact, I will be the one trying to interview her."

"Want backup? I'm free tomorrow," Nora offered right away, her eyes sparkling. A vision of her in her push-up bra sprang uninvited to my head.

Chloé protested. "Pick me, darn it! I haven't had a chance to help yet."

I looked at her quizzically. "After last winter, when you were dating the one who ended up being the murderer, you still want to be involved?"

She grinned sheepishly. "Okay, but I'm over it now. And I'd really like to help. Anyway, wouldn't Nora going with you look weird?"

"I suppose you're right," Nora grumbled. "I'm not exactly escort material anymore, am I?"

I was still debating whether or not I wanted anyone with me, but finally decided that having Chloé along might not be a bad idea. I reluctantly agreed and we made our plan for the next day.

———

Of course, other than arriving on time, nothing went according to plan. First, she brought Bentley; I insisted that he remain in the car. I could just imagine the scene if we'd brought him up to the escort office. As it was, just as the elevator doors parted and we were about to step out, I spotted Elizabeth entering the reception area. My arm instinctively shot out to push Chloé back inside the elevator, and I quickly followed and pressed the 'close door' button. Chloé looked at me with eyebrows raised and mouth ajar.

"That woman with the long blonde hair is the woman that I think tried to run over Milton yesterday!" I exclaimed. "Why is she here? She's connected to all this, I'm certain." I groaned in frustration. "There are so many strange circumstances, yet I'm certain that it's all connected."

"You'll figure it out, Mali. You always do."

"I don't know this time…"

"I'm guessing we're not going in, right? So why don't we go back to your place, write down all the weird little things we do know, and then see if we're any further ahead?"

I nodded sullenly.

Once we were back outside, I quickly called to cancel my appointment with Madame, saying that I was having doubts about this being the correct career choice for me, and thanking her for their time. Between Elizabeth's sudden appearance there and the receptionist dating Eli, I didn't think it would be safe to rebook.

After a quick trip to Tim Horton's for a French Vanilla coffee and a Boston Crème donut (which Bentley tried to lick), we returned to my place and I dragged out the large easel I'd purchased several months ago. Chloé took the marker from my hand, smirking and shaking her head. "I can't let you write, Mali. You know we'll never be able to make out a single word!" Sadly, she was correct. Even my best handwriting was awful and resembled chicken scratches. "Alright, tell me what you know." With a marker in one hand, and Bentley tucked away in the crock of her other arm, she began to write as I rambled. Hummer glared from across the room, displeased with the company at hand.

"Milton gave Blanche his salad, at her request. Blanche dies within the hour. While Milton was walking, he is run off the road. He's later almost run off the road while in his car here at the bistro. He is convinced that someone wants to kill him. Many people would probably like to kill him. Blanche was a former escort, and met Milton at the agency. She'd previously dated Mr. Gregson, who was also at the bistro that night. Mrs. Gregson also formerly worked as an escort. Elizabeth was going into the escort agency today. Is she an escort? She worked for, and slept with, Milton, then suddenly quit, saying she'd found another job. Elizabeth possibly also has ties with Eli. I'm sure it was her at his place. Is she into drugs? Blanche also dabbled in drugs, perhaps, at Elis' place, who, by the way, happens to be a fairly significant drug dealer and suspected to be in the Lebanese Mafia…"

I momentarily lost my train of thought. Suddenly, I wanted a beef Shawarma sandwich. The Lebanese always made the best pita sandwiches.

"Focus, Malia!" Chloé snapped me back to reality, also startling Bentley into a barking fit.

"Where was I? Oh, yes. And Eli is dating the escort agency's receptionist. What else?" I searched my memory. "Greg Gregson was still pining over Blanche, so it seems, and hated Milton with a passion. Poisonous plants were in the salad that Blanche ate, disguised as part of the salad, and these same plants could have come from my little garden. Hmmm, and pesky Leonardo knows of this little garden and still bad-mouths me. But who would have been able to come in here and put poisonous plants in the salad, and known that it was going to be given to Milton, or to Blanche? That's the part that maddens me."

Chloé looked at me sadly before speaking. "You often forget to lock the back door; someone could have slipped inside…" I sighed in response. Yes, I do. "But again, how could they have known who that plate would go to? Maybe it comes back to Mr. Gregson being here that night. He'd also come the next day and was looking around for something he claims to have lost. Wait, was he here before or after Milton had ordered? Oh, for the life of me, I'll never remember that." I slapped myself on the head in frustration. The clue was here somewhere. Literally here, at the bistro. But what was it?

"It's no use, Chloé. We're no further ahead. Let's go have a shawarma. I need to clear my thoughts."

She grinned and grabbed her purse. "You don't have to ask me twice!"

It took ten minutes to drive to the nearest shawarma place, our mouths watering the entire time. As we entered, I was surprised to see the old lady that lived next to Milton, Mrs. Knuedle, sitting at a booth alone, staring intensely at the servers. Or perhaps she was just starring into space (that tends to happen with old people). I glanced at the servers myself, and not noting anything out of the ordinary, walked the few remaining steps and placed my order. Chloé did the same, and as we waited for our food to be prepared, I caught the sound of a heated discussion coming from the kitchen, just behind the servers. I perked up an ear, but the voices had fallen. Quicker than I could turn my head, Eli came charging out from the kitchen, stormed through the small restaurant and out the front door. I looked at Chloé in shock, and then caught sight of Mrs. Knuedle quickly leaving as well, a half-eaten shawarma clutched in her hand. What was the old biddy up to?

All this seemed to make even less sense than everything that had gone on before. We settled ourselves at a table, and as we unwrapped our sandwiches, I quietly told Chloé about Eli and Mrs. Knuedle, since she hadn't met or seen either of them before and would not have noticed or understood the significance of what had just transpired. "I think we can add this little incident to the list on the easel! Yes, there's definitely something odd about old Mrs. Knuedle."

The germ of an idea began to form at the back or my mind.

Chapter Twenty-Three

We returned to the bistro, added the new information about Mrs. Knuedle to the easel, and mulled over the list again, still with no success. I wasn't ready to share my thoughts about the Knuedle incident yet, but I would be paying her a visit soon.

"Hey, I almost forgot. I have a present for Bentley!" I pulled out a little doggie-sized t-shirt for the dog, advertising the bistro. It was a cute little number that boldly stated the bistro's name and "Mad Dog". Yes, a wine, of course, and hilarious on little Bentley who always had a mischievous smile on his furry little face.

Chloé bundled him up in his new shirt as she squealed with amusement. "Okay, we're ready for action. What's next, Mali?"

"For you, nothing else today, Chloé. I appreciate your help this morning, but we're done for now, and I think that Bentley is ready to go home." The truth was that I didn't want to have to worry about the dog barking in the car and drawing attention to us, or worse, leaving him at my place to terrorize the cat and crap all over the floor.

Chloé took her leave, since she wasn't working that evening, and I began to prepare the evening's hot dish. I would be making a chicken and fusilli pasta dish with a sun-dried tomato Alfredo sauce, four cheeses and a sprinkling of bacon. Although I'd just eaten, my mouth watered again. Dammit! No wonder I was putting on a bit of weight.

Beth, Nicole and Billy were soon on hand to help for the evening. Once things quieted down, I left Nicole in charge while I quickly changed into jeans and a plain t-shirt, along with a ball cap, under which I tucked my hair. I was hoping not to be noticed since I had some slinking around to do. The three could easily manage without me now that the rush was over.

I drove quickly towards Milton's house, wanting to have enough time to investigate before the sun set. First, I stopped at his house to drop off his platter, having called him earlier to let him know I'd be in the area. Then, I parked alongside the road, about six houses further onward, and backtracked on foot, pretending that I was just a neighbor, out for an evening stroll. Nothing stirred at Mrs. Knuedle's house—I would get to her in due course. I glanced up the driveway toward the pervert's house, but didn't see any shadows lurking in the window. Milton's house appeared calm from the outside, and I pictured him munching happily on his food. Finally, I approached Eli's house and my pace slowed.

Glancing about, I did not see anything out of the ordinary, no other cars parked at the side of the road, nothing that seemed to indicate that there was any surveillance going on in the neighborhood. I couldn't help wondering if Rick and Matt had been fibbing to me about Eli being in the mafia and under surveillance, just to scare me off the case. Bending over, I retied my perfectly tied shoelaces, casually glancing about to see if I could spot any vicious dogs or cameras. Again, all seemed very quiet.

Too quiet, in fact… I had hoped to see some cars in the driveway, and hoped to catch a glimpse of who would be coming and going from his place, preferably Elizabeth, or someone who might look familiar and then the whole case would neatly fall into place. But that didn't happen. I not-so-nonchalantly walked by a half dozen times before sensing that I wasn't alone anymore.

Seemingly out of nowhere, I felt a presence behind me. I picked up my pace but couldn't shake the feeling. I bent suddenly to tie my laces again, hoping to catch a glimpse of who was behind me, and before I could react, I was scooped up by a firm grip around my elbow and dragged several paces before being shoved next to a tree. "What are you doing?" Mrs. Knuedle snarled at me. "Are you trying to get yourself killed?" I stared at her in confusion, wondering where her strength had come from and noting that she no longer had a limp. Come to think of it, she had moved awfully quickly at the restaurant earlier that day, too, when she had scooted after Eli.

Yes, it suddenly made sense! An old lady living alone in a big house with very few personal effects... I was positive that my hunch was correct: she was the detective that was handling the surveillance. Who would ever suspect a feeble, old lady? Except she wasn't so feeble, and maybe not that old, either... She saw the comprehension on my face. "Come on, busybody, let's go over to my place." She resumed her fake limp as we walked.

Once inside, I was seated uncomfortably on her plastic-wrapped furniture again. Of course, it was borrowed furniture, hence the reason for the plastic covers. "So, what were you hoping to accomplish out there, other than getting yourself in trouble?" she asked.

"I've been hoping to find Blanche's killer. I'm close to solving the mystery, I'm certain of it. How long have you been watching Eli?" I asked in return.

"Long enough to know that he has nothing to do with the murder. He's clean, we can't seem to pin a thing on him."

"Well, I know he deals drugs," I boasted.

"Oh, we know that, but he keeps things on a very small scale here. He's not dumb enough to get caught with anything significant at his home. We've been trying to figure out who the main players are, where he goes, who he hangs with, where the real hub is located. We can't have someone like you walking back and forth a dozen times, making him think he's being watched. He's bound to slip up eventually, and I can't have you risking the whole operation by bumbling around."

"Hey, I wasn't bumbling!" I grumbled. Well, maybe I was bumbling, a little. "What about the restaurant? It seems to me that would be a good place for a main hub, as you call it. People are always coming and going from there, so any extra foot traffic by dealers or buyers wouldn't be as noticeable, I would think. Is that why you were there today?"

She sighed, her patience running thin. "Yes, that's why I was there today. You'd do well to stay away from there. He's bound to recognize you eventually, between your visit to his home, his trip to your bistro, your trip to the escort agency, and you slinking around today."

I gasped. "How do you know all this?" She simply glared at me in response. I tried a different tactic. "Fine, can you tell me anything about Milton and Blanche then?"

"The intended victim was Milton, not Blanche. I've lived next to them long enough to know that. Everyone liked her, but he's a mean old turd."

"I know that already. But did you ever notice anything weird going on at their place?"

"I was told that they had parties now and then, but there haven't been any since I moved into the neighborhood. She'd sometimes go over to Eli's place, but she wouldn't stay long and she'd always leave alone or with female friends. Heck, even the pervert across the street would go to those parties sometimes!" She chuckled.

"Is he harmless? I mean, he's always there in the window, watching. Could he have been obsessed with Blanche?" It hadn't occurred to me before, but having asked the question, it suddenly seemed feasible.

"I suppose that's possible," she agreed, pursing her lips. "I think, though, that if he were involved, that after her death, he would have wanted to lie low rather than continue to draw attention to himself. My guess is that he gets his jollies by prancing around naked inside his home, looking out the window, and going to the door naked if some unsuspecting person happens to ring his bell." She snickered, remembering that Beth and I had been unsuspecting people who happened to ring his bell. "Listen, if you want to investigate him, be my guest! I won't stop you. Just stay away from Eli's place."

We sat in silence for a few minutes. I hadn't given this man much thought, until now, and I became increasingly suspicious the more I thought about him. Was he my missing link? "All these people know each other," I mused aloud. "Blanche, Eli, the pervert, Elizabeth, who I believe is the one that tried to run Milton down twice, in fact. She used to work for Milton. Maybe there's more to this. Does the naked man have many visitors?"

She shook her head. "He mainly just stands in the window, looking out."

"Looking out. Looking out," I mumbled to

myself. "Looking out!" I suddenly exclaimed, making her frown.

"Yes, that's what I—" She stopped abruptly. "Of course! You're right!" She stared at me in amazement. "Well, this doesn't help your case, but it certainly helps mine. He's the hub! He's Eli's lookout-man! That's why we haven't been able to spot anything—he's on to us! His man watches the area, knows if I'm here or not, or if anyone else is lurking about, and keeps Eli informed. He's not a pervert, like we've all been led to think, he's a decoy! Brilliant! I don't think he's involved in the murder in any way, but he's certainly involved in my case."

"What's at the back of his yard?" I asked. "Is there some other access to his house, other than the driveway?"

Her eyes sparkled with excitement. "There must be! You have to leave now; I've got things to do." She quickly escorted me to the door, and then hesitated. "You can't just simply walk out of here and then walk a few houses to your car. If he's watching, it will look weird. Let me get the dog and we'll make this look good."

She hurried to the second floor of the house then returned with her dog in tow. "I keep him upstairs in one of the spare rooms when I'm out of the house," she explained. "I'm quite allergic to dogs, but it's been a great cover, out walking the dog, being a nosy old lady. Oh, don't get me wrong, I'm quite fond of the pooch, but he's not mine. Borrowed, just like the rest of the house and furniture. Okay, here's what we'll do. We'll go out to walk the dog together, and you can then slip away in your car. If anyone's watching across the road, they won't see your car where you left it, and if we're lucky, he'll just assume you're a neighbor from further down the street. Let's hope this works. He's obviously realized that I'm a detective, but that doesn't mean we want to draw attention to you. Follow my lead carefully," she ordered with a stern look before opening the door.

She ushered me outside then followed, resuming the limp. At the end of the driveway, I started to head right as she went left. "Thank you so much for the visit, dear," she called out. "That was so nice of you to check on me. I'll just walk the dog quickly then turn in for the evening. Take care!"

We parted ways and I made it safely to my car. I didn't dare head back in that direction, so I continued down the road and took a longer way home. On a hunch, I travelled down one street over and slowed in the area where I thought the look-out's house might be. It was hard to pinpoint, especially as the sun had now set, but there were some empty properties in the area, one of which only had a dirt road cutting through it, deep into the treed lot. Could that be the access point to the spotter's house?

I stepped on the gas and sped by, always paranoid about drug dealers and cameras; this was not my case, though I did feel a swell of pride at having possibly helped to crack it. I hurried back to the bistro, eager to share my findings with someone. Only Nicole was still there, doing the last of the clean-up and waiting anxiously for me, her face relaxing as I rushed in and locked the doors behind me.

She gave me a curious look. "Were you at Milton's this whole time? Have you succumbed to his charms?!" She knew that I had brought him his platter and couldn't resist poking fun.

"I had another stop to make. I ran into his neighbor, whom you haven't met yet, and we got to talking. She's a yappy old lady…" I didn't offer further information. Nicole hadn't been very involved in this case, and as this portion of it seemed unrelated to Blanche's murder, I thought it best to keep it to myself. In any case, it had been a long day and we were both eager to have it end.

Chapter Twenty-Four

With no new leads to investigate the next day, I decided to visit a few more people on the list that Milton had given me. Dad was my sidekick again, but only because I was fairly certain we'd be in no danger. I was right; after a few hours of gentle snooping, we were no further ahead, the list of suspects quickly dwindling.

With some poor timing on my part, we became ensnarled in rush-hour traffic. An eighteen-minute drive was well on its way to taking an hour and a half. I was lucky to get hold of Beth, who was already at the bistro, and asked her to start preparing the meat and cheese platters, including one for Milton. Luckily, I had already put several things into slow cookers that morning, for the evening hot meal, so I didn't have to worry about that.

I arrived just as Beth was wrapping Milton's platter and as Billy and Chloé sailed in through the back door. To my dismay, Bentley was also present. At the sight of all of us, he squirmed in excitement and escaped from Chloé's arms, landing on Milton's half-wrapped platter and clambering his way up the front of Beth's shirt to give her happy licks on the cheek.

"Damn it, Bentley, look what you've done," she cussed, agitated by the contaminated platter and swiping at the slobber he'd left on her cheek. I wasn't too happy myself as the platter would now have to be redone. Chloé attempted to reclaim her pet, who was now standing on Beth's shoulder, attempting to make his way over to Billy, who was standing close by.

In the midst of this chaos, Billy suddenly decided that this was the perfect time to finally ask Beth out on a date. In response to his question, her head whipped around in his direction, knocking Bentley gently on the nose by accident, who retaliated by nipping at her hair just as Chloé lifted him back into her arms. To everyone's amazement, a long, dark, mass remained clamped in Bentley's mouth. He escaped from her arms again, leaping to the floor with his prize and violently shaking it with all his might. Billy stood still, his mouth open with shock, as he waited for a blonde-haired Beth to respond to his question. Her ebony hair had been a wig and suddenly everything fell into place. This was the missing link, the AHA moment, when everything suddenly made sense.

She glanced wildly in my direction, saw the comprehension register on my face, then sprang into action, sprinting towards the front of the bistro to make her escape. Unfortunately for her, my brown and yellow hero, my dad, was in her way, his cane accidently catching her feet just enough to send her sprawling. Leaving the wig behind, Bentley ran to her, thinking that she wanted to play. While giving her wet kisses, she tried to fend him off and get back on her feet.

"Get her, Dad!" I shouted. He looked at me in confusion and I quickly said the word "killer" in Hungarian. He responded with an agility I hadn't seen in years by springing into action and whacking her behind the legs with his cane while I yelled to Nora, who had just walked in, to call 911.

She sprang into a ninja position, sensing all the activity, and froze in that position, unsure what to do next. "911!!" I shouted while throwing myself onto Beth's back. "Beth is the killer!" I finally yelled in English.

She struggled under me as my father added his fly-weight to the mix and sat upon her legs. Bentley was still furiously trying to lick her face and Billy looked like he was still waiting for a response to a request for a date. I could hear Nora in the background, finally on the phone with a 911 dispatcher, asking for help and proudly declaring, "We've caught a killer!"

Just as she hung up the phone, Milton entered by the back door. He observed the scene for a moment, shrugged, and then asked if his food was ready. "No!" I shouted, "Throw that platter out!" It had just occurred to me that Beth had prepared it, knowing full well that it was for him, after already having tried to poison him once. She started shouting wildly, not having seen him from her position, but recognizing his voice.

The yelling and cursing continued as Milton made his way over to where I sat upon a wild and enraged human who wished him harm. He gasped when he saw her face. "Elizabeth. What are you doing here?" Beth was none other than our Elizabeth Wagner, who used to work for him and had tried to run him over. As she continued to scream, I raised my voice so that he could hear. "She's the killer, Milton. That's how the poison got into the salad. She knew that you liked the salad here, so she got a job here and waited for her opportunity. Of course, she was familiar with the plants in my garden, as she used to take her smoking break out there. I'm guessing that she chopped and mixed the poisonous plants together and waited for her chance to use the mix. Unfortunately, you and Blanche switched salads, and since Blanche had been ill recently and on antibiotics and low on potassium, her death was fast. Had you eaten it, it may have taken longer, and you likely would have died hours later, or possibly become very ill." I had done more research on the various plants and how certain poisons worked. "Of course, I could be wrong," I added.

"Very good, Ms. Kis! Very good indeed!" a voice boomed. The police had arrived and I was happy to see Officer Lynette, already familiar with the case. I could see Officer Sean behind her and gave him my usual sneer. "That sounds about right, from what I overheard." She grabbed Beth's hands and cuffed them behind her back, and then she and Sean helped her to her feet and out the back door to where the police car was parked.

We all stared at each other in silence for a moment. "Vat de heck?" my father finally exclaimed, sinking onto a nearby chair, his knees suddenly weak. I rolled my eyes.

"I'm not going into accounting, Dad, so don't even say it!" Everyone, including him, burst out laughing. I turned to look at him and was surprised to see him grinning. The old coot was enjoying himself! I grinned back. "Good job, Dad!"

Chapter Twenty-Five

It was strange to have wrapped up a case and not have Matt there to tie up all the loose ends. I felt a pang of sadness at the thought, but I had learned enough from him to be able to summarize everything myself.

We had all given our statements to the police, then opened the bistro and took care of the hungry crowd. Milton had eaten out on the front porch, finally at peace and no longer in fear for his life. To my surprise, I noticed Greg and Lea Gregson sitting with him; surprised on two counts, actually. First, that they had come to my bistro after knowing I had been helping to investigate, and second, that they were sitting with Milton and appeared to be amicable.

"What was that about?" I asked Milton after they left, joining him on the porch with a freshly opened bottle of Fat Bastard. I had grown to like him, so the choice of wine was purely accidental. He chuckled as he helped himself to a full glass.

"It seems that Greg has come to his senses. He was civil, and offered his sincere condolences about

Blanche. He and Lea shared news that they were adopting a child. They seemed quite excited. I think they just wanted to share the news with somebody, even if it was me. He's too old, if you ask me. Lea's quite a bit younger than him. I'm not sure what she ever saw in him." He snickered to himself and I smiled, having wondered the same thing about Blanche and Milton a dozen times, if not more. Love works in mysterious ways.

We sat in comfortable silence, drained by the events of the day. Our view was not spectacular, as it looked onto the parking lot, but the air was warm and soothing, the breeze gentle, as darkness began to fall. We drank deeply from our glasses, both feeling happy that everything was back to normal.

The sound of tires on the gravel stirred me from my thoughts and I smiled widely once I recognized Nathan's jeep. Although thoughts of Matt had stirred a certain sadness in me, Nathan made my heart skip a beat and my smile wider than I'd ever thought possible. I excused myself and met him halfway, both of us rushing just a little bit until we were in each other's embrace.

"Can you spare a few minutes?" Nathan asked. "I have some news to share with you." I didn't much like the sudden serious look on his face.

"Sure, let's go up to my place. Everything is under control here, so they won't need me until closing time." I said goodbye to Milton after getting him to promise that he'd visit me every once in a while then led Nathan up to my home. Hummer sat on the coffee table, staring at us as we settled on the couch. He seemed to nod, as if to say, "*You may proceed.*"

"What's the news?" I inquired, suddenly afraid to hear the answer.

He grinned. "I got a promotion!

"That's great!" I exclaimed, relieved that it was good news. "Congratulations! When do you start?"

"In a few weeks… But I have more news. I have to move, Amalia," he said quietly, his eyes boring into mine, concerned. "The job is in Kingston." My mind raced. Kingston was two hours away.

"What does this mean?" I asked softly. *Mean for us*, I meant to say, but those were all the words that I could choke out. He ran his fingers through his curly hair.

"Ever think about moving?" he asked.

"What do you mean?" I stammered. Was he asking me to move with him?

"Listen, I know it's crazy, we didn't meet that long ago, but every moment I've spent with you has been gold. I think we get along so well, I'm crazy about you, and I don't want this to end. I'll drive two hours here and back to see you every day that I can, but maybe, you know, maybe you'd consider moving… with me?"

"I would love to, Nathan, but I have the bistro here, and my parents moved here to be close to me. I wasn't expecting anything like this." My voice faded.

He pulled me close, kissing me gently on the

forehead. "I understand, I do. It was just a thought. Like I said, I still want to be with you. If necessary, then I'll drive to the moon to see you. And whenever you're off work, you can come to spend time at my place, if you like," he added hopefully.

"Of course, I'd like that!" I replied quickly. "I'm usually off three days in a row. You might get sick of me, you know."

"Never," he replied, giving me a long kiss.

I walked him back to his jeep, gave him a lingering goodnight kiss, and then joined the rest of my friends inside the bistro in time to tidy up. Once everything was in order, we sat at our favorite spot and all eyes turned to me, waiting for answers. Nicole was there too, having come in after Nora had called to tell her that Beth had been discovered to be the killer.

"Okay, here we go!" I said. I knew that everything I had to say would make sense once my breath returned after Nathan's kiss, and once my aneurism stopped twitching, and I was able to speak again.

Chapter Twenty-Six

"Beth's real name was Elizabeth Wagner, and she worked for Milton. She'd had an affair with him, and he'd give her money, which she used to feed her drug habit. Nothing hard-core, but she had a rather expensive cannabis habit of close to a thousand dollars a month. I heard from Officer Lynette earlier, who told me that Beth had confessed. She had hoped that Milton's heart would give out while they were having sex. Since he was old and out of shape, no suspicion would be aroused. He'd told her that she'd be in his will if she stayed on as his lover, and she apparently believed him. Although I'm somewhat fond of Milton now, I can't say I approve of how he's conducted himself in the past. In any case, I guess one day she just snapped."

I went on to explain how she had applied for a position at the bistro, knowing that Milton and Blanche occasionally dined here. She had poisoned Milton's salad, but he'd given it to Blanche when she wanted to switch because his had more strawberries.

And Beth had been eager to help me with the investigation so that she'd know if she had anything to worry about.

"What about Eli and the mafia?" Nora asked. "Was he her drug dealer?"

"I believe so," I started to answer then broke off suddenly as a knock sounded at the front door. I rose to answer it and was surprised to see Matt and Mrs. Knuedle standing there. I invited them inside and once everyone was seated, I turned to the unlikely pair. Matt averted his eyes.

"Do either of you have anything you can share with us about Eli?" Matt nodded his head at Mrs. Knuedle who broke into a grin.

"You were right, Amalia. Mr. Balzak, the man across the street who played the role of a sexual voyeur, was Eli's front man and would handle the bulk of the drug deals. Although we never saw people coming and going from his place, there was an alternate entrance, a trail leading through the woods to his backyard. Since the lot where the trail started was uninhabited, the foot traffic didn't arouse any suspicion. It was quite brilliant, really. Your friend Beth actually ran drugs for Eli from time to time, doing drops and collecting money. Of course, she used drugs too, as we now know. While Beth was being arrested this evening for her crime, we also swooped down on Eli and Mr. Balzak and made quite a drug bust. Both men will likely go to jail. It also appears that Eli had ties with the escort company where Lea and Blanche worked. We're not sure to what extent yet, as we're still uncovering all the details, but it seems that he may actually have been the owner."

"What was that Mr. Gregson looking for that time he was here, Amalia?" Nicole asked this question, referring to the time after Blanche's murder when I'd caught him looking around the patio.

I sighed. "I asked Officer Lynette to look into that. I suspect, however, that he'd simply dropped a joint and had been looking for it. I found one on the ground earlier that day, and I guess he was a little embarrassed. I could be wrong, but I'm fairly certain about that. From what I hear, both Milton and Greg used to have wild parties back in their younger days."

"You're probably right, Amalia. From what we understand, the drugs flowed freely via the escort agency," Matt continued. "It was all about having a good time."

He and Mrs. Knuedle took their leave shortly thereafter. Matt gave me a warm, though slightly sad, smile, and congratulated me on solving the case. "As always, you came through. Take care of yourself, Amalia." And with that, he was gone.

Nicole was next to leave. "Sorry, folks, but I'm bushed. I was on a date earlier today with Drew and have another one with him tomorrow, so I need my beauty rest." Her face lit up as she said his name

Nora rose too. "I have to get going, too. I told Craig I was returning home tonight, so he'll be worried that it's so late." My jaw dropped at the mention of her husband.

"No more Mr. Leonardo?" I asked.

"I don't think so…" She exhaled the words, along with a sigh. "As much as he drives me nuts, I just can't seem to end my marriage with Craig. Can't live with him, can't live without him, I guess. Maybe it's just hormones triggering my mid-life crisis, but I think I'll get some counselling and figure things out once and for all!"

Soon, everyone but my dad was gone. We sat there, grinning at each other, a first in our relationship. He looked proud, and energized. "We make a pretty good team, Dad. Thanks for being there to help me." I gave him a big hug and was pretty sure that his eyes went misty. "Did you tell Mom?"

"Yes, I told her. She wasn't happy with me and called me an old fool. She says if I can run around with you solving crimes, then I can take a polka dancing class with her…"

"Better you than me, Dad. Just make sure she doesn't accidentally sign you up for pole dancing, like she did to me." I gave him a big kiss on the cheek and sent him home. "Thanks, Dad. Now go on home and rest."

I locked up, triple checking everything as I usually do, but without the feeling of fear that I often had, then made my way up to my living quarters. Hummer wrapped himself around my legs, demanding attention and his midnight treat.

"I hear you, I hear you!" I opened his can of smelly

food then sat on the ground with him, watching him eat. Once finished eating, he began to clean himself, a contented smile on his face. I gave him a few tar-tar-control treats to make his breath tolerable, and to butter him up for our talk.

"So, what do you think about us moving…again?" I asked him. He paused in mid-lick then blinked before returning to the task at hand.

"Yeah, I didn't think you would approve," I replied. "But that doesn't positively mean it won't happen…" he looked at me and yawned, butted his head against my knee, and then took off down the hallway toward my room, ending the conversation. "…one day!" I finished.

"What was that real estate agent's name again?" I mused out loud. Yes, Janet Reno. My hand first hesitated, and then quickly composed a text. With a long breath, a pregnant pause, and a huge smile, I tapped the "send" button.

Chicken Fusilli

- 2 skinless chicken breasts or 4 deboned, skinless chicken thighs

- 2 cups Fusilli pasta

- Creamy garlic alfredo type pasta sauce, plus add a ½ teaspoon garlic powder (or make your own – see below) plus 1 teaspoon mustard

- 1 regular size can of diced tomatoes

- 1 small can of mushrooms (whole or pieces, whatever you prefer)

- 1 teaspoon olive oil

- Selection of cheeses, grated

- Bacon, diced and cooked

Dice chicken. Heat olive oil in pan on medium high, then cook chicken until done. Set aside.

Combine pasta sauce (and garlic powder and mustard), tomatoes and mushrooms. Simmer on medium high heat for about 20 minutes, giving flavors a chance to marry. Sauce will likely be tasty as is, however, you can also add herbs of your choice for extra flavor.

Cook pasta according to directions. When ready, drain, serve with sauce and top with cooked chicken. Also good with grated cheese of choice (pop into microwave for about 45 seconds to melt cheese to perfection) and a handful of cooked bacon.

If you just want a creamy garlic sauce, omit adding canned tomatoes. Mushrooms are also optional.

Home-made creamy garlic sauce

- 1 cup milk
- 1 cup water
- 1 teaspoon cornstarch
- 1 teaspoon garlic powder
- 1 teaspoon mustard
- ½ teaspoon salt
- Few shakes of black pepper (about ¼ teaspoon)
- Few shakes of paprika, if you have any (¼ teaspoon)

Combine all of the above in a saucepan and cook on medium heat. Mix with a whisk every few minutes so that cornstarch is well blended and sauce doesn't stick to bottom. Once sauce begins to gently boil, reduce heat. Simmer until sauce thickens. If too thick, add more milk. If not thick enough, mix more cornstarch (1/2 teaspoon) in a glass with some cold water before adding to hot sauce. Add can of tomatoes and mushrooms as noted above.

German Oven Pancakes

This is a just a bonus recipe. I usually like to include recipes that are mentioned in book, however, this one is simply a recent addiction that I had to share. The consistency is like a custard or almost cheese-like, and the flavor is simple but yet so good. I found several variations of this recipe on Pinterest, went with the easiest version, and really the only thing I changed was using almond extract instead of vanilla and using cooking spray on the casserole dish instead of a ton of butter. I hope you enjoy as much as I do. In fact, I enjoy it every two weeks or so!

- 9x13 inch glass baking dish works best
- 4 large eggs
- 2 cups milk
- 1 teaspoon almond extract
- 1 and 1/3 cups flour
- 5 tablespoons white granulated sugar
- Cooking spray

Heat oven to 400 degrees.

Combine all the ingredients and blend well with electric mixer. Spray a large casserole dish with cooking spray, then pour batter into dish then bake in oven for about 20-25 minutes until the edges are puffy and a nice golden color. Remove from oven and dust with powdered sugar, then serve immediately; the consistency is like a firm custard.

Slice and serve with a nice fruit topping, maple syrup or a squeeze of lemon. Keeps well in fridge. Reheat slices for a minute in the microwave.

Acknowledgements

Special thanks, as always, to my son Kyle and my life-partner Paul, two incredible men that I love dearly and who keep me grounded and sane. Whatever life hands you, be strong.

Thank you, also, to all my readers, friends and fans, and to Kelly and David at Open Books for their patience, kindness and understanding. I am so lucky to have found a home at Open Books.

RIP to my buddy, Hummer. You were a good cat and I'm sorry I couldn't be there when you passed away.

This book took over two years to write. Sadly, during that time, my dad, Julius Volhart a.k.a Mr. Kis, passed away on February 15, 2017, the day before my cancer diagnoses. Although he was very proud of me for being published, to my knowledge, he never read my books and did not know that one of the characters was inspired by him. I never told him. *Bazd meg.* RIP, Dad.

This past year brought some uncertainties regarding my own health; a battle with stage four kidney cancer was never part of my plan. I went from an initial prognosis of 22 months to an amended one of five years, which will hopefully change again to ten or twenty years. I had thought that Amalia and her friends might take a little break, but after about a month of mulling it over and trying to find a purpose in life, I jumped right in and started book four. Stay tuned for *Swiss Cheese and Sibling Rivalry*, which will be published sometime in 2018.

Cheers, my friends,
Judy